P

CARLTO]

"Easily the craziest, weiı
writer in America."
—*GOTHIC MAGAZINE*

"Carlton Mellick III has the craziest book titles... and the kinkiest fans!"
—CHRISTOPHER MOORE, author of *The Stupidest Angel*

"If you haven't read Mellick you're not nearly perverse enough for the twenty first century."
—JACK KETCHUM, author of *The Girl Next Door*

"Carlton Mellick III is one of bizarro fiction's most talented practitioners, a virtuoso of the surreal, science fictional tale."
—CORY DOCTOROW, author of *Little Brother*

"Bizarre, twisted, and emotionally raw—Carlton Mellick's fiction is the literary equivalent of putting your brain in a blender."
—BRIAN KEENE, author of *The Rising*

"Carlton Mellick III exemplifies the intelligence and wit that lurks between its lurid covers. In a genre where crude titles are an art in themselves, Mellick is a true artist."
—*THE GUARDIAN*

"Just as Pop had Andy Warhol and Dada Tristan Tzara, the bizarro movement has its very own P. T. Barnum-type practitioner. He's the mutton-chopped author of such books as *Electric Jesus Corpse* and *The Menstruating Mall*, the illustrator, editor, and instructor of all things bizarro, and his name is Carlton Mellick III."
—*DETAILS MAGAZINE*

"The most original novelist working today? The most outrageous? The most unpredictable? These aren't easy superlatives to make; however, Carlton Mellick may well be all of those things, behind a canon of books that all irreverently depart from the form and concepts of traditional novels, and adventure the reader into a howling, dark fantasyland of the most bizarre, over-the-top, and mind-warping inventiveness."
—EDWARD LEE, author of *Header*

"Discussing Bizarro literature without mentioning Mellick is like discussing weird-ass muttonchopped authors without mentioning Mellick."
—*CRACKED.COM*

"Carlton is an acquired taste, but he hooks you like a drug."
—HUNTER SHEA, author of *Forest of Shadows*

"Mellick's career is impressive because, despite the fact that he puts out a few books a year, he has managed to bring something new to the table every time... Every Mellick novel is packed with more wildly original concepts than you could find in the current top ten *New York Times* bestsellers put together."
—*VERBICIDE*

"Mellick's guerrilla incursions combine total geekboy fandom and love with genuine, unbridled outsider madness. As such, it borders on genius, in the way only true outsider art can."
—*FANGORIA*

Also by Carlton Mellick III

Satan Burger
Electric Jesus Corpse (Fan Club Exclusive)
Sunset With a Beard (stories)
Razor Wire Pubic Hair
Teeth and Tongue Landscape
The Steel Breakfast Era
The Baby Jesus Butt Plug
Fishy-fleshed
The Menstruating Mall
Ocean of Lard (with Kevin L. Donihe)
Punk Land
Sex and Death in Television Town
Sea of the Patchwork Cats
The Haunted Vagina
Cancer-cute (Fan Club Exclusive)
War Slut
Sausagey Santa
Ugly Heaven
Adolf in Wonderland
Ultra Fuckers
Cybernetrix
The Egg Man
Apeshit
The Faggiest Vampire
The Cannibals of Candyland
Warrior Wolf Women of the Wasteland
The Kobold Wizard's Dildo of Enlightenment +2
Zombies and Shit

Crab Town
The Morbidly Obese Ninja
Barbarian Beast Bitches of the Badlands
Fantastic Orgy (stories)
I Knocked Up Satan's Daughter
Armadillo Fists
The Handsome Squirm
Tumor Fruit
Kill Ball
Cuddly Holocaust
Hammer Wives (stories)
Village of the Mermaids
Quicksand House
Clusterfuck
Hungry Bug
Tick People
Sweet Story
As She Stabbed Me Gently in the Face
ClownFellas: Tales of the Bozo Family
Bio Melt
Every Time We Meet at the Dairy Queen, Your Whole Fucking Face Explodes
The Terrible Thing That Happens
Exercise Bike
Spider Bunny
The Big Meat
Parasite Milk

STACKING DOLL

CARLTON MELLICK III

ERASERHEAD PRESS
PORTLAND, OREGON

ERASERHEAD PRESS
P.O. BOX 10065
PORTLAND, OR 97296

WWW.ERASERHEADPRESS.COM

ISBN: 978-1-62105-265-4

Printed in the USA.

AUTHOR'S NOTE

People often ask me which book of mine is my favorite, but I never know how to answer this question. I have written over 50 books since the late nineties and each one of them is my favorite for at least one reason. I think *Dairy Queen* is the cutest, *Apeshit* is the goriest, *Clusterfuck* is the funniest, *Clownfellas* was the most fun to write, *Zombies and Shit* was the most exciting to write, *Handsome Squirm* was the most uncomfortable, *Egg Man* was the most satisfying, *Satan Burger* made my career, etc. But my usual answer for this question tends to be *Quicksand House,* because it's one book that I'm very proud of and it has been a reader favorite ever since it came out in 2013. It's not really my favorite book, but it's the closest I've had to a favorite ... until now.

Stacking Doll might not be the longest or weirdest or most ambitious book I've written, but the second I finished it I knew it was going to be my new favorite. I'm a sucker for love stories, especially dark surreal love stories, and this is by far my favorite love story that I've written. I had a smile on my face from beginning to end and couldn't wait to share it with the world.

I'm excited as hell for you to check out this book. I hope you like it as much as I do. If you don't, that's okay, I love you anyway. I'll try harder next time. But if you do like it you'll be my new best friend. We can go to Tokyo and eat pickled lemons while listening to Turkish dance pop in a swan-shaped hot air balloon. Or just get beer and pizza. Whatever works for you.

—Carlton Mellick III 3:22 pm 6/11/2017

For Rose

CHAPTER ONE
YNARIA

Her favorite food is tomato pizza with bacon and strawberries. Her favorite lipstick is plum pie-flavored. Her favorite movies are comedies where people die. She thinks it's funny when people die.

She has porcelain white skin that glistens like it's wet and glossy in the sunlight. Her painted-on purple eyes are like gemstones that twinkle when she smiles at me. She has hair like black licorice, dark rubbery locks that smell of clove and anise.

Of all the women I've dated, I've never known anyone quite like Ynaria. She's not exactly human, but she's the only woman for me.

"You're getting married?" Mark says, sitting at the table with a beer in his hand that he hasn't even touched since I dropped the news. "Seriously?"

"You're a fucking idiot," Rick says, sitting next to him. He guzzles his beer to near completion.

I knew this would happen when I told my two best friends about my engagement to Ynaria. They've never exactly approved of me having any kind of serious relationship. The idea of getting married, ever, to anyone, at all, is like blasphemy. I hoped taking them out for beers would soften the blow, but it's going just about as badly as I expected. Or maybe a little worse.

"So fucking stupid..." Rick adds, shaking his head.

"You've got to be joking," Mark says. "Tell me you're joking."

"I'm not joking," I tell them. "This is what I want."

"But you're only twenty-three," Mark says.

"Twenty-four," I correct him.

Mark says, "Whatever, it's still crazy. If you were in your thirties I'd understand. I'd still think you were an idiot, but I'd understand."

"Your parents had three kids by the time they were my age," I say.

Mark ignores my comment. "You've only been with her for a year. You haven't even lived together yet. At least move in with each other for a few years. You don't really know a person until you've lived together for a few years."

"I don't want to wait," I say. "I know for a fact she's the one I want to be with."

"Bullshit," Mark says. "I've been madly in love with girls a dozen times before. I've been with girls I was convinced I wanted to spend the rest of my life with. But you know what happened? That feeling went away. *Every. Time.* I grew to despise every single girl I've ever fallen in love with. Trust me, you're making a mistake."

Rick stays quiet, just nodding his head at every argument Mark gives.

"This is different, man," I say. "She's absolutely everything I want in a woman. She's perfect."

Mark bursts into laughter. "Yeah, you say that now. That doesn't last. You probably love every little quirky flaw about her. But eventually the love fades. Her quirks will go from cute to annoying. And she'll stop putting up with your bullshit. No more drinking with your friends. No more video games. No more leaving your underwear on the floor. And you'll grow to resent each other for it."

I shake my head. "You don't know her like I do. She's not like that. She's not like normal girls."

"That's the problem," Rick says, breaking his silence to interject. "She's *not* like normal girls."

I stare at him, wondering what the hell he means by that. Rick pauses to pour himself another beer from the pitcher. Then he chugs half of it.

Rick belches and stares at me with a grim face. "If Mark isn't going to say it, I am. The *real* problem is not that you're getting married. It's that you're marrying a fucking *nesting doll*."

Mark and I cringe at his words and look around the bar to see if anyone heard him say that.

In a quiet voice, I say, "Don't be so racist."

Rick raises his voice. "I'm not *racist*. If she was black or Mexican or Asian, I'd have no problem with it. But nesting dolls aren't human. They're *things*. You might as well be marrying a robot or a dog."

He's never said it out loud, but I've always suspected that Rick had a problem with the fact that I was in love with a nesting doll. Not a lot of people are comfortable around nesting dolls. They only make up one percent of the population, so a lot of people, especially people from rural areas like where Rick grew up, haven't had a lot of exposure to them. They think they're weird and frightening. Some people even think they're evil. Demonic. And the idea of human/nesting doll relationships is still considered a sin to some people.

"A dog?" I say. "Are you seriously comparing Ynaria to a dog?"

Rick shakes his head, knowing he went a little too far. "Look, I have nothing against nesting dolls. I think prejudice against them is bullshit and I don't even have a problem with you dating one. But marriage is a different story. Think about what your life will be like. Think about what that will do to your children. Do you really want to put them through that? Nesting doll/human hybrids have it worse than anyone. They won't be accepted by humans *or* nesting dolls. People will think they're freaks."

I just lower my eyes and shake my head. I have no idea what to say to him right now. I kind of want to punch him in the face.

"He's kind of got a point," Mark adds.

I look up at Mark. I expected this behavior from Rick, but not him. He was the one who introduced me to Ynaria in the first place.

Mark explains himself, "Look, I like Ynaria. I think she's cute. She's fun. I don't have a problem with nesting dolls. But you'll have to put up with all their weird customs. You'll have to raise your kid like a nesting doll kid. She's religious, isn't she? You'll have to go to their weird churches. They don't even eat or bathe like normal people."

"So what?" I say.

"It's just that humans and nesting dolls are *really* different," Mark says. "Even if you're emotionally compatible, you're not going to be culturally compatible. Not to mention all of her layers. You wouldn't just be marrying her. You'd be marrying all the people who live inside of her. Have you ever even met any of her other layers?"

I shake my head. "They're private. She'd only let me see them if we were married."

"You see," Mark says. "You have no idea. She could have crazy people living in her. It's just too weird."

I shrug. Since all the people that live inside of Ynaria are what make her who she is, I'm sure I'd love them just as much as I love her.

"Not to mention, you'd be marrying *that*," Rick says, pointing to an old nesting doll woman as she walks into the bar.

Mark and I turn to look at her. She is a jar-shaped babushka doll, her limbs and face appear as though painted onto her body. She wobbles across the floor, eyeing us as she moves. Unlike Ynaria, she looks exactly like a Russian nesting doll, like the antique toys. But she's huge, bigger than a human. She's a living, breathing wooden doll.

"You really want to fuck *that* the rest of your life?" Rick asks.

I shake my head at him, disgusted at the thought of Ynaria becoming like that.

"Hell no," I say. "But she won't be one of those until she's an old lady. And besides, everyone is gross once they get old. You don't marry someone based on what they'll look like when they're seventy."

"Still, though…" Rick says. "Knowing that she'll eventually turn into *that* would give me nightmares. I couldn't do it."

"Well, I'm not you," I say.

He just shakes his head and lets out a loud sigh, then drinks his beer.

"There's got to be *something* we can say to get you to change your mind," Mark says.

"There's not," I say.

Mark says, "What if we promised to get you laid every Friday for the next two years? Would you leave her for that?"

I shake my head.

Rick says, "What if I made you a partner in my company?"

I shake my head.

Mark says, "What if I tracked down that girl you were in love with back in college?"

I shake my head and say, "I can't believe you guys."

"We're not giving up," Mark says.

"We know what's best for you," Rick says.

But there's nothing they can say to change my

mind. I let them go on for the rest of the night, but it only leaves them feeling depressed and defeated. They never congratulate me or even pretend to be happy for me. They're convinced that once I get married they'll never see me again.

Ynaria wants me to meet her parents tonight. I'm dreading the thought of confronting them, especially after she told me that they're even less approving of our marriage than my friends. She spent the whole night getting a lecture about why humans and nesting dolls shouldn't marry. They told her everything my friends said to me, about how our cultures are too different, about what it would be like for our children, trying to convince her that she's making a huge mistake. And Ynaria responded by telling them that they would change their minds if they met me. She thinks they'll like me immediately. She doesn't realize what kind of pressure that puts me under.

I pick up Ynaria in front of her apartment.

"Are you ready?" she asks, lifting her fluffy white doll dress and hopping into the passenger seat.

"Of course," I say, lying through my teeth.

The red circles on her cheeks glow pink with excitement and she kisses me on the chin with her firm doll lips.

"I just know they'll love you," she says, wiping purple

lipstick off of my face.

I nod my head. Her unwavering optimism is one of the reasons I love her so much, even when it's completely unrealistic. From what she's told me about her parents, them being strict traditionalists without an open-minded bone in their bodies, I doubt they'll like me one bit.

"But why did you wear this?" she asks, pulling on my brown suede jacket. "You should have worn a Matryoshkan suit. They would have liked that."

"I don't have any Matryoshkan clothes," I say.

I also have no intention of dressing like a 17th century Russian school boy. Ynaria might look good in doll clothes, but they would make me look like an idiot. Even Matryoshkan guys wouldn't be caught dead wearing them.

"Well, you're going to need some for the wedding," she says.

I pull away from the curb and head into traffic, so focused on driving that I almost missed what she just said to me.

"Wait…" I say. "I'm not wearing a tuxedo?"

"Of course not!" She laughs and punches me in the shoulder so hard I wince. Besides her skin being harder than a human's, she also punches with the force of seven fists. Even a playful tap on the arm will cause a bruise. "We're having a traditional Matryoshkan wedding. You can't wear a tuxedo."

I rub the pain out of my shoulder. "When did we decide we'd have a Matryoshkan wedding?"

"I'm the bride," she says with a plum-colored smile. "I get to decide on the wedding. You get to decide what we'll do for the rehearsal dinner, the second brunch, and maybe the honeymoon ball, if you want."

I say, "Wait… second brunch? Honeymoon ball? What's that?"

"Matryoshkan weddings are seven days long," she says. "There are multiple events we'll have to plan for. The honeymoon ball happens the day after the wedding. It's kind of a second reception dinner, where the family celebrates our departure to our honeymoon."

I'd never heard of this before. I knew Matryoshkans were very festive people, but I had no idea they put so much into their weddings.

"Huh…" I say. "Sounds expensive…"

"Oh yeah. *Really* expensive." Ynaria nods her head with giddy enthusiasm. "There's a joke my people make about why Matryoshkans never remarry—our weddings cost too much to have more than one in a lifetime."

I smile at her but don't make a comment. Meeting her parents already has me in a panic. I don't need something else to worry about, like how much debt Ynaria and I will accumulate before we even start our lives together. I hope she knows that my parents have absolutely no money to contribute whatsoever.

We arrive at Ynaria's family home just before dark. They live in a nesting doll neighborhood, near the Matryoshkan shops and restaurants on the east side of town. Her parents run an antique store known for having the rarest collection of wooden dolls in the Northwest. Tourists from all over the country come to see their collection. Long before I met Ynaria, my family used to take me there to look at the dolls as a child. But they'd never buy me one. They were far too expensive and not really meant as children's toys. I always thought they were neat, though—especially when I learned they were designed after a real race of people.

"Straighten your shirt," Ynaria says as we get out of the car.

I straighten my shirt as I step onto the driveway.

"Fix your hair," she says, brushing my bangs out of my eyes.

I pat down my hair, doing the best I can to comb it without a mirror or a comb.

"Smile," she says. "You're not smiling."

"Why would I smile?" I ask.

"You're meeting my parents for the first time," she says. "You should be excited."

"But I'm nervous," I say. "What if they don't like me?"

"They *won't* like you if you don't smile."

I put on an obviously fake smile as she rings the doorbell.

Ynaria looks at me and says, "Stop smiling. You look like a crazy person."

So I stop smiling.

She locks her arm around mine, posing like somebody is about to take a picture of us. When the door opens, a large jug-shaped babushka doll appears in the foyer. My mouth drops open in shock when I see her. I didn't know Ynaria's mother was old enough to have a rounded outer shell. She is taller than me by about a foot. Her body is so wide it barely fits through the doorway as she steps forward and lets her daughter give her a big hug.

"Ynaria," she says. "You look so lovely tonight."

Ynaria just smiles at the compliment as her mother admires her frilly white dress.

"This is Benjamin," Ynaria says, pointing at me. "He goes by Ben, but I like to call him Benny. He hates when I call him Benny."

Then she pushes me with all of her strength at her mother, catching both of us off guard. I land with my arms around the rotund doll as though I meant to embrace her. She doesn't make a sound. It feels like she's holding back a cringe, as though human flesh is awkward to touch. But it's even stranger to me. I've never felt the skin of an old nesting doll before. It's hard as wood and cold against my skin. It feels like I'm hugging a giant egg. I try not to think about how Ynaria will one day look exactly like this.

"Hello," I say when I separate from the babushka doll. "It's very nice to meet you."

The babushka doll just clears her throat and waddles backward. She couldn't look more displeased to meet me.

"Yes," she says. "Ynaria has told us about you."

I nod and smile.

"Come with me," she says.

Then she turns and waddles deeper into the house.

When her mother's back is turned, Ynaria pinches my hip and glares at me.

"Why didn't you hug her longer?" she whispers in an angry tone. "You're blowing it."

I just shrug at her in confusion, not sure what the hell she's talking about. Her mother seemed annoyed that I hugged her at all.

The house is filled with flowery orange wallpaper, antique lamps, yarn draperies, and shelves full of little wooden dolls. It feels like I'm walking through my grandma's attic, or maybe a tacky German restaurant.

I am seated at the dining room table across from an old Matryoshkan man. He doesn't introduce himself. He just stares at me. Like the mother, he has the large ovular body of an elderly nesting doll. He doesn't sit in a chair. There's no need. The bottom of his body is flat. The middle of his body does not bend.

"We didn't know what you eat, so we got you McDonald's," says the father, gesturing toward the bag of fast food on the table. "You people always seem to like McDonald's."

I open the fast food bag. There's a Big Mac and french fries. It's all cold and hard. It seems as if the food was purchased earlier in the day or maybe the night before. I wonder if it's safe to eat. There's also a goulash-like dish—noodles, pickles and beef stewed in a spicy sauce—in the center of the table that was made for the rest of them. It smells delicious.

"You didn't have to go through the trouble of getting me something special," I say. "I eat Matryoshkan food all the time."

Ynaria says, "He doesn't eat fast food. He thinks it's too salty and fattening."

The father coughs in annoyance, then glares at me for being ungrateful. I look down at my lap.

As Ynaria serves herself the saucy casserole, she looks over at me and says, "You can have some of mine."

I nod at her. I really don't want to eat a cold Big Mac.

She eats half of her food before serving me. It's okay though, I'm a little too nervous to eat anyway. I can see all the rows of teeth in her mouth as she chews, feeding all seven of her bodies. It reminds me of the creature from the *Alien* movies. The extra rows of teeth are the only sign of her inner bodies.

"This is great, Mom," she says to the babushka woman.

The mother smiles and pats her head against her daughter's shoulder.

Then there's silence for a few minutes as the family eats. The sound of dozens of mouths smacking echoes throughout the dining room. I eat the small portion of casserole Ynaria gave to me. To not be rude, I add some McDonald's french fries to my plate, just in case they are offended that I won't eat the food they bought just for me. But when the parents see me mixing french fries with their homemade Matryoshkan dish, they are even more offended than if I would have eaten nothing at all. I try to ignore their angry faces.

To break the awkward silence, I say to the father, "Ynaria says you run the antique shop on 23rd street. I've been there many times. My parents used to take me there as a child."

The father just grunts at me. Ynaria looks at me in shock like I just did something horribly offensive. I wonder if Matryoshkans don't talk at all while eating. Or maybe it's rude to mention a person's business at the dinner table? Who knows…Ynaria hasn't prepared me at all for what I should and shouldn't do around her parents.

The father drops his fork to his plate and wipes his mouth in frustration.

"Now that I've lost my appetite…" he begins. "I'm going to be straight with you…"

As he says this, I can't help but wonder why he lost his appetite. Was it something I said, something I did? Or is it just the idea of eating in the presence of a human that disgusts him?

"I think what you and Ynaria are planning is absolutely ridiculous," he says.

I put down my fork. I was half-expecting what is

about to come.

He continues, "I have five sons, but only one daughter. I'll be damned before I allow her to marry a human, especially one as ill-mannered as you."

"Daddy!"Ynaria screams, pounding her fist on the table with such strength it nearly cracks the wood.

"I'm just speaking frankly, Ynaria," he says to his daughter. "Even humans respect frankness." He turns to me. "You wouldn't want me to hide my feelings would you, Young Man?"

I realize there's still a bite of food in my mouth. I swallow it with a loud gulp. Then I respond, "Of course I wouldn't."

"Good," he says, then smiles with contentedness. "You see, you're both very young. You don't fully understand what you're doing. A simple fling between a human and a Matryoshka is no big deal. But marriage is a completely different matter. You have no idea what it means for our people to intermarry."

He pauses, waiting for a response. I'm not sure what he expects me to say.

I tell him, "My friends gave me many reasons why I shouldn't marry Ynaria. But I don't—"

He cuts me off."Then they are very good friends. I strongly suggest you listen to them."

The man is beginning to frustrate me. I don't know if it's the adrenalin built up from the stress of the situation or what, but I find myself unable to control what I say next.

I put both of my hands on the table as if I'm ready

to stand up and get in his face. "Look, I know it won't be easy. But I don't care. I love Ynaria. I *know* we're right for each other. There's no other person I'd rather marry."

Ynaria smiles when I say this, but her parents scowl in disgust. Her mother's mouth widens in revulsion. Her father bites his lip with an inner set of teeth. Then the father chuckles at me and shakes his head in a smug, superior way.

"You don't even understand what it means to love a Matryoshkan," he says. "You don't just love the person on the surface. You must love all the people inside of her. Every single one of them. If you don't then it's not true love."

The father moves toward a liquor cabinet and breaks open a bottle of wine. He pours himself a tall glass and takes a drink.

"It's easy to love the outer layer of a woman," he continues. "It's the most beautiful layer. It's the one she wants to show the world. But it's not who she really is."

He returns to the table. "Do you know why I laughed when you said you loved my daughter?"

He waits for my response, but I just stare blankly at him.

He says, "It's because you haven't even met her yet. It's ridiculous to say you love a person you haven't even met, isn't it?"

I look at him for a moment and then break eye contact. I don't know what to say.

"I'm sure you know that she has many people who

live inside of her," he says. "But did you also know that she will grow new layers as time goes by? She will become a new person, with a new name, a new personality, new interests and desires. This will happen two or three more times in her lifetime. If you marry, you won't just be marrying her. You will marry all of the people inside of her and all of the people she will eventually become. If you were Matryoshkan then it would be okay because you would go through the process together. But because you're human, you will never change. You will remain the same person until the day you die. With each new layer, you'll have to fall in love all over again. This is not something a human could possibly understand."

After the father's speech, there is a long pause of silence. The mother smiles with satisfaction, feeling the father's words were finally getting through to us. Even Ynaria just slinks down in her chair with a frown on her face, wondering if her father might be right.

I know that if I don't say something now it'll all be over. I'm not sure what I can say to debate her father's points, but I can't just give in. I love Ynaria too much to let her go.

I stand up and look at the father. I stare into his flat purple eyes.

"It doesn't matter," I tell him. "Maybe I haven't met Ynaria's other layers, but I couldn't imagine loving them any less than I love her. If they are a part of her, I know I will love them with all my heart. And so what if she changes into new people as she gets older. Even humans change with age. I'll love her no matter who she is or who she becomes. And not you or anyone else is going to change my mind about that."

The father laughs at my words and a sudden chill crawls up my spine. I can't believe I said that to him. I feel so embarrassed. And I bet Ynaria is so pissed at me for yelling at her father that she'll never forgive me. But when I look down at her, she's not angry at all. She's smiling at me with tears in her eyes. That's when I realize I've just confessed my love for her in such a way that I've never done before. By saying this, I've convinced her that our marriage is really what is best for us, that it is worth fighting for.

When Ynaria stands up and yells at her dad, he stops laughing.

"I can marry whoever I want," she tells him. "I'm an adult now. And I'm marrying Benny whether you like it or not."

The parents gasp at their daughter's outburst. Then they glare at me as though I'm to blame for her disobedience.

The mother yells something in Matryoshkan at Ynaria, something like *Sit down this instant, Young Lady!*

She immediately returns to her seat and pouts. Then she stabs her fork into her food. I decide to sit down as well.

"Very well," the father says in a much calmer tone. "If we can't persuade you to see reason with our words then we have no choice but to accept your decision."

"Really?" Ynaria asks.

I nod my head. "Thank you."

The father adds, "As long as you still feel the same way about each other after The Trial."

I look at Ynaria. I have no idea what he's talking about. Ynaria just smiles when her father mentions The Trial. Her mother, on the other hand, has a look of horror on her face. It's like she can't believe the father would even suggest such a thing.

He says to me, "I can tell by the look on your face that Ynaria has not told you about The Trial."

I shake my head at him. "What is The Trial?"

"It's a Matryoshkan custom," he says. "Upon engagement, a couple must go through The Trial to see if they are truly compatible with each other."

"Dmitri…" the mother says to the father, shaking her head in a panic. "Don't even joke about this. They mustn't."

But we both ignore her words.

"I don't understand," I say. "What kind of trial?"

The father smirks at me. "You will be locked away together for several days. At least a week. Perhaps longer. Some trials last months."

"Is that all?" I ask, not sure what he's getting at.

The father ignores my question. He continues, "During this time, you will get to meet all of Ynaria's layers. You will spend at least a day with each one. You will get to know exactly who you will be marrying, right down to her core."

I look over at Ynaria and she grabs my hand,

squeezing it tightly. I can tell her parents are disgusted by the show of affection in front of them.

Her father continues, "You said that you will love my daughter no matter what her inner selves are like. This will be your chance to prove how much truth is in your words. If you still wish to marry my daughter after The Trial is over, I will bless your union completely."

I squeeze Ynaria's hand.

"That sounds fair," I tell him. "I'll go through this trial. But I promise you that it won't change anything. I know I'll love her inner selves as much as I love her."

The mother interjects, "A human's never done The Trial before. We have no idea what will happen."

The father smirks and says, "That won't stop Benjamin here, will it?" He looks at me. "You'd do anything to prove your love for Ynaria, wouldn't you?"

"Of course," I say.

He nods. "Then it's settled. I'll get everything prepared. Contact your employers and let them know you'll need some time off of work. The Trial will begin next week. Let's say Friday."

"Sounds perfect," I say, and smile at Ynaria. She smiles back at me. Her cheeks glow a brighter pink than they ever have before.

When Ynaria and I get up to leave, the father approaches me. He pushes me into a corner with his big round body and says, "Know that I tried to help you. The Trial wasn't meant for human eyes. Whatever happens, I won't be held responsible. It's all on you."

"What is that supposed to mean?" I ask.

But he doesn't respond. He turns to his daughter and she lets him give her a big hug goodbye. She looks happier than I've ever seen her before. It's too bad that her parents don't share even the smallest bit of their daughter's happiness.

The whole ride home, Ynaria can't take her hands off of me. She tears open my shirt and kisses my neck.

"What's gotten into you?" I ask, but don't tell her to stop.

"I can't believe we're really doing The Trial," she says, then she licks the side of my face. "I didn't think we'd get to because you're human. You'll get to see me. *All* of me. It's going to be so romantic."

"How come humans don't go through The Trial?" I ask. "Plenty of humans and Matryoshkans have married before. How come they never do it?"

It takes a few minutes before Ynaria answers, busy sucking on my ear and pulling me toward her as though she's trying to get us into a car accident.

Once she pulls away, she says, "Humans usually only marry non-traditionalists and half-Matryoshkans that don't follow our customs. And these days, a lot of Matryoshkans tend to hide their inner selves from their spouses. They hide their inner layers from even themselves, as though they're scared of them. But I like the idea of you getting to meet the people inside of me. I want you to love them just as much as you love me, just like you said you would. I never expected you to, but it means so much to me that you will."

I nod at her, but I'm not quite sure what she's talking about.

She lays her head on my shoulder and says, "My parents were wrong about you. You really *are* different from other humans, just like I thought you were." She rubs her abdomen as though she's connecting with the people inside of her. "They can't wait to meet you. They'll love you just as much as I do. I know they will."

As she closes her eyes and snuggles into the crook of my neck, I wonder exactly what I'm getting into with this trial. The old man made it sound kind of terrifying. It made me wonder what exactly lives inside of Ynaria. No human has ever seen a Matryoshkan's inner layers before. What if they are hideous? What if they are made of blood and guts? What if they turn out to be exactly like the demonic hellspawns that hardcore Christians always claim that they are?

While I turn a corner, an old hippie cyclist races across the street. I swerve to avoid him, but the car next to me isn't quick enough. It plows straight into the cyclist, crushing the bike under its wheels. The old hippie smashes into the windshield and is thrown over the roof of the vehicle.

Ynaria opens her eyes just as the cyclist is tossed into the air. At first, her face lights up with shock, but then a cheerful smile curls on her lips. She busts into laughter, laughing at the top of her lungs and pointing at the old hippie as his body collides with the asphalt, like she's watching some kind of slapstick comedy.

"Oh my God!" she cries, pointing at the cyclist's crumpled up body. "Look at him! There's blood everywhere!"

Ynaria won't stop laughing as I pull over. The lady in the car that hit the cyclist is in a panic, wondering if she killed the old man. She turns to us and sees Ynaria laughing and slapping her leg.

"He's still alive," Ynaria screams in delight. "Look at him trying to crawl away! He's gagging on his own blood! He looks so stupid!"

More people pull over to help the man. A couple in the car behind us are calling an ambulance. A group of college guys block off the road so that nobody else hits the injured man.

As the crowd thickens, they all start to notice what Ynaria is laughing at.

"He thinks he's going to live!" Ynaria laughs. "Look at him try to live!"

I become completely embarrassed. I know it's illegal to drive away from the scene of an accident, but I decide that it's best for everyone that I get Ynaria far away from here. There's enough people here to help the man who was hit.

As I pull away, Ynaria slaps at my arm, "No, don't leave yet! I want to see him die! It's going to be hilarious when he dies!"

But I don't listen to her and continue on down the road. I just hope nobody takes down my license plate number.

"He'll be fine," I say. "I'm sure he'll get to a hospital in time."

Ynaria keeps laughing. She tries to calm herself, but still snickers beneath her breath every other minute. I knew that she thought death was funny in movies. Sometimes her laughter was inappropriate, like when she laughed at all the battlefield scenes in *Hacksaw Ridge*. But I never saw her laugh at real people getting seriously injured before, especially an injury as serious as the cyclist back there, who very possibly could have died. I wonder if she'd feel the same way if something like that happened to me.

When she notices the upset look on my face, she stops snickering and says, "I'm sorry. I know it's mean. I just couldn't help it. It's the Vera in me. She has a morbid sense of humor."

Then she kisses me on the neck and lays her head on me again.

"You'll meet her soon," she says. "You'll understand once you meet her."

I just nod, wondering what the hell I've gotten myself into by falling in love with this nesting doll woman.

CHAPTER TWO
VERA

I spend the entire week both excited and scared shitless about doing The Trial with Ynaria. On one hand, it sounds like a vacation, a week-long pre-wedding honeymoon. On the other hand, I'm terrified that I won't like her inner selves. I'm worried that her father is right about us, that we don't belong together. But I love her too much to back out of it. No matter what happens, I'm seeing this to the end.

It wasn't easy getting an indefinite amount of time off of work. My boss gave me all kinds of shit for it. He didn't even believe The Trial was a thing. I explained that it was a law to let me have paid leave to do it. He tried arguing that I'm not Matryoshkan so it didn't apply, but the law doesn't state that I have to be a nesting doll to get the time off. As long as I'm marrying a nesting doll, it's fine. But when I left work today, he still treated me as if The Trial was some kind of elaborate plan to take a lot of time off, no matter how much paperwork I showed him.

He said, "If I wanted to deal with bullshit nesting doll customs, I would have hired one."

But that just made me smirk. I wonder if Ynaria

had to go through the same shit with her employer.

When I get to the address Ynaria gave me, I see a large concrete building with no windows and only one door. It's covered in decades-old graffiti and barbed wire. It doesn't look like anyone's stepped foot in there for a very long time.

I pull my car over on the side of the road and notice several nesting doll people from Ynaria's church gathered out front. Three of them are bringing in jugs of water and supplies from the back of a van. A young bald priest with circular glasses and a gray clipboard seems to be in charge, directing the others on their tasks. He somehow recognizes me the second I get out of my car.

"Benjamin Hammond?" he calls out to me in a thick Matryoshkan accent, waving his clipboard.

I step forward and say, "Yeah, that's me."

He smiles and introduces himself as he shakes my hand, "Father Adrik Plokhov. Wonderful to meet you."

"Likewise," I say and return the smile.

Unlike Ynaria's father, this priest seems much more pleasant and friendly. I was expecting someone on the judgmental side.

"It is very honorable that you and Ynaria have agreed to go on The Trial," he says. "Young couples have been straying from this tradition more and more these days. It's a shame, really. Our customs are dying and it's important that we keep them alive, now more than ever."

I nod at him, then look around, trying to see if Ynaria is here yet, hoping that she'd save me from this conversation. She said she would come right after work, but I don't see her anywhere.

Father Adrik continues, "But you two will set a new example for young couples in our congregation, especially considering your lack of a Matryoshkan bloodline. If a human is willing to do The Trial then it creates a new precedent. It's revolutionary. Everyone at our church is very excited."

He smiles and leans in so close I can feel his cold breath against my forehead.

"Yes, well…" I clear my throat and take a step back. "I'm happy to help. Ynaria is really looking forward to this."

He nods rapidly. "I'm sure she is. It's a very intimate experience. You'll get to know each other inside and out." Before I can open my mouth to comment, he changes the subject. "By the way, if you pass The Trial and marry, can I expect to see your family in our church? We are very progressive at Sacred Heart Chapel. Humans are very welcome. Some of our sermons are even in English."

I just smile and say, "I'll have a talk with Ynaria about that."

"I know you people like rock and roll," he says. "Our choir knows a few rock and roll hymns. I'm sure you'd love it."

"That sounds great," I say, nodding slowly. "Thanks for the invitation."

"Of course, of course," he says.

I look around again. "Has Ynaria arrived yet?"

"She's inside the sanctuary, unpacking," he says.

"Thanks."

But before I can go for the entrance to the building, the priest gets in my way, blocking my path.

"But we have some business to attend to first," he says, holding up his clipboard. "I need to go over the contract."

"The contract?"

He nods. "Yes. It is a legal agreement stating that our church will not be held responsible for anything that happens to you during your trial. Ynaria will also not be held responsible for the actions of her inner layers, even when said actions result in injury or death."

"Injury or death?" I ask. "Is it really that dangerous?"

The priest shrugs. "It's just a precautionary measure. Very few people are killed during The Trial. But it happens from time to time. You might not know this about Matryoshkan physiology, but our inner layers are much different from our outer layers. They are personifications of all the deep, hidden layers of our psyche, the parts of ourselves that we don't let out into civilized company for good reason. They act on impulse and emotion. They say and do whatever is on their minds. They don't hold anything back. Without our outer shells keeping them at bay, they would be uncontrollable. They would be a danger to society."

His words make me far more nervous than I was before. I begin to wonder if I'm actually ready for this.

"Are you serious?" I ask. "Nobody told me any of that before."

He realizes how nervous he's made me and tries to

calm me down.

"It's nothing you should worry yourself about," he says. "Forget that I used the word *dangerous*. It's rare for them to be dangerous. *Unrestricted* is a better word to describe them. You might find that some of her inner layers have racist or sexist feelings toward you and won't be afraid to share them. You might find that one of her layers has unusual sexual desires that she would have been too afraid to reveal to you in her outer form. You might learn that parts of her are much stranger and more unattractive than you ever could have expected."

"And one layer might be a homicidal maniac?" I ask.

I'm thinking of Vera, the inner woman Ynaria mentioned that has a morbid sense of humor. She laughed when that old cyclist nearly died in the street. She thinks death is funny, *real* death. I don't know if I like the idea of being locked in a building with her for a week. She's the one that worries me the most.

The priest clears his throat. "It's possible, but not likely. One in a million. I really wouldn't worry about it."

He holds out the clipboard and I find myself signing without reading a single word. I guess Ynaria is worth the risk.

"Let me see your cell phone," he says.

I hand it to him. He immediately programs in an emergency contact.

"Call this number if you want to cancel The Trial," he says. "I'll come by immediately to let you out."

I nod at him as he hands me back the phone.

"But be warned, if you call before The Trial is over, no matter what the reason, then you both fail," he says. "You will never be permitted by our church to undertake The Trial again. Your union will not be blessed by God."

"What if there's an emergency?" I ask. "What if I break my leg or get seriously ill?"

He smiles. "Well, that would be a real test of your relationship, wouldn't it?" He puts his clipboard under his arm. "There are no exceptions. Just finish The Trial. Decide if you truly love her right to the core. Only then will you be able to marry."

I just stare blankly, not sure what to say. All I know is that, for Ynaria, I'm willing to go through anything.

"That's why so many young couples forgo The Trial these days," he says. "They are too scared of what they might find. But if you ask me, that's not true love. It's not true love if you don't accept your spouse for everything that they are."

Then the priest steps away, sighing with joy as he returns to the other Matryoshkans. I didn't see a wedding ring on his finger. I wonder if he's ever been through The Trial himself. I wonder how many nesting dolls do it at all.

Three bags and two suitcases in my hands, I enter the building, searching for Ynaria. Unlike the decrepit exterior, the inside is very nice and clean. The place is large with high ceilings and wide open rooms. Everything is white and sterile. The walls, the furniture, the stairs, even the lights—all white without an ounce of color.

Two men don't make eye contact with me as they unload groceries into the kitchen cabinets and refrigerator. Another man in a maintenance outfit comes up from the basement and joins them.

"I got the power going," he says.

When he sees me looking at them, he breaks eye contact and goes quiet. I'm wondering if it is customary for them not to interact with the couple before their trial or if it's because I'm human. The looks on their faces seem to say *poor bastard...* But I think that might just be my imagination.

Ynaria comes down the stairs wearing a new purple dress that matches her plum-flavored lipstick. The bright color of her outfit contrasts with her white surroundings, drawing my eyes right toward her. She must have bought the dress just for this occasion. I couldn't imagine her being more beautiful on our wedding day.

Her eyes light up when she sees me. One smile is all it takes to melt all of my worries away.

"You look stunning," I tell her, suddenly feeling underdressed in my work clothes.

"You look terrified," she teases."You must have spoken to Father Adrik."

I nod. "He had me sign the waiver."

She laughs.

When she gets to the bottom of the stairs, she wraps her heavy arms around my waist and kisses me. I drop all of my luggage to the floor and pull her closer. Then she buries her face in my neck, tears of anticipation forming on my shirt.

"I can't believe we're doing this," she says. "It's so unreal."

"Well, your father didn't give us any other choice," I say.

She looks up at me. "I'm glad."

"Me, too."

I'm not sure, but that was very possibly a lie.

She doesn't let me go, clinging to me as she speaks. "So what do you think of the place?"

I look around the room and say, "It's really… *white*."

She snickers. "Yeah, it's tradition. The sanctuary is always colorless and boring. It's so that we put all of our attention on each other instead of our surroundings. There's no internet, no television, no distractions of any kind."

"Sounds fun," I say.

"Oh, it *will* be."

"Is that your car out front?" Father Adrik asks from the doorway.

I nod and walk toward him.

"This is a really rough neighborhood after dark," he says. "You won't want to leave it out there for the whole trial."

"How rough are we talking?" I ask. "Are we going to be safe in here?"

He smiles and nods his head. "Oh, *you'll* be fine. Nobody can get in or out of the sanctuary. But I can't say the same for your car." He holds out his hand. "Give me the keys. I'll park it somewhere safe and return it to you once The Trial is over."

I take the keys out of my pocket and hand them to him. "Alright."

"So this is it," he says. "Are you both ready?"

"Definitely," Ynaria says.

The priest looks at me. "Ready as I'll ever be, I guess."

He smiles. "I'll take that as a yes."

"It's a yes," I confirm.

"Very well…" He lets out a sigh. "Then may God bless you both. Good luck to you."

Before we can say goodbye, he closes the door in my face. The sound of hammering echoes through the wood as the men on the other side board up the door, sealing us both in.

"Is that really necessary?" I ask Ynaria, wondering why the hell they need to board up the place.

"It's tradition," she says. "We have to be completely locked in and unable to escape. No cheating."

I nod, but am still not completely sure that explains it. "Seems a little extreme."

"Matryoshkans take their customs very seriously," she says.

"I've noticed."

I spend an hour unpacking my bags and changing into more comfortable clothing. This place is going to take time getting used to. It feels like a cross between a resort and a hospital. The iridescent lighting is hard on my eyes. It reminds me of the lighting in elementary school classrooms, radiating from the ceiling, reflecting off of every surface of the room, including the white tile floor.

The place smells funny. At first, I thought it was some kind of chemical, like bleach or cleaning fluid. But it's something else. A candle wax odor. Unscented candle wax. I'm not sure where it's coming from, but it's everywhere. All over the white blankets and pillows, on all the doorknobs, inside the dresser drawers. It's not exactly disgusting, but not pleasant either.

Downstairs, I find Ynaria pouring us two glasses of champagne, ready to toast the first day of our trial. She hands me a flute and chimes the rim.

"Cheers," she says.

I take a sip and watch her. I don't say anything, just admire every detail of her porcelain white skin. I love how Matryoshkans have such smooth skin. They don't have pores like humans. They rarely have any blemishes or imperfections, outside of the occasional chip or scar. Ynaria's only chip is on one of her toes. She's only showed it to me once. She's very embarrassed about it. Nesting doll skin might be harder and less flexible than human tissue, but it makes them more beautiful, at least to the eyes. The touch takes a little getting used to.

"Did you talk to your parents about this?" she asks.

I shake my head. "I couldn't get a hold of them."

Ynaria looks at me, almost upset by this news. "Do they even know we're getting married?"

I look down. "I'll talk to them after The Trial."

"They do approve of us, don't they?" she asks. "It won't be like my parents, right? We don't want to go through this for nothing if they won't bless our union."

"They'll be fine with it," I say. "They're in a polyamorous relationship with a younger man. They don't have a traditional bone in their bodies."

"Oh…" she says, almost disturbed by my response.

"I've emailed them pictures of you when we first started dating," I say. "They said you were really pretty. They didn't even seem to notice you're Matryoshkan."

"Oh…" she says, still disappointed in my words for some reason.

I drink my champagne and pour another glass.

"You don't talk about your parents a lot," she says.

I shrug. "I don't really get along with my parents."

She looks at me with a dead serious face. "Were they mean?"

I laugh and wave her words away. "No, not at all. Self-absorbed is how I would describe them. Both are artists. They cared about their work and their art friends far more than they cared about me. I was more of a decoration than their child. Sometimes I feel like they had me just to add something wholesome to their biography."

Ynaria nods. I'm not sure she knows what I mean.

"Aren't they French?"

I laugh and take another sip. "They *wish* they were French. They moved to Europe the day I went to college, without saying a word, and haven't been back since. I got to visit them once, a few years ago, when they were staying in Prague. But it was unbearable. They're more pretentious than ever."

Ynaria nods and looks down. Then her eyes dart back up and she says, "They must be rich."

I laugh again. "They're artists. They only pretend that they're rich."

"I hope they come to our wedding," she says.

I finish my drink and push the glass away.

"I hope they don't."

"So are you ready to get started?" Ynaria asks.

We're both buzzed and loosened up. I almost forgot that we're on The Trial.

"Get started?" I ask.

She nods. "I want to show you my next layer."

I pause, hesitating, not quite ready to get into that.

"Already?" I ask.

She nods and smiles with her big purple lips.

"I thought we'd spend the first night getting used to the place. There's no rush, is there?"

The smile falls from her face.

"But I'm really excited for you to meet the rest of me," she says. "Aren't you excited?"

"Yeah," I say, trying not to hurt her feelings. "I'm just nervous."

"I'm nervous, too," she says. "Let's do it."

I nod. "Okay."

She faces me, her hands trembling. It reminds me of the first time we made love, the first time we saw each other naked. She removes her dress. The light reflects off of her porcelain skin so brightly that I have to shield my eyes. I've seen her naked many times before, but it's always a surreal experience every single time. The licorice-black hair in her crotch and armpits is flat and smooth against her skin, appearing as though it's painted on. Her nipples are light gray and almost indistinguishable against her paper-white breasts. She doesn't have a belly button like humans do, but there is a crease in her abdomen right where a belly button should be. It is the line that separates her top half from her lower half.

"I'm going to open up now," she says, then lets out a nervous giggle.

I just nod, unable to speak.

She massages the crease in her abdomen, rubbing it until it becomes moist. A lubricating fluid leaks from the crack. When the opening is wet enough, she puts her fingers inside and then slides her legs off like a pair of pants. A smaller pair of legs appears beneath. They are just as pale, but are definitely not hers. Just by the feet I can tell that they belong to somebody else.

There's a tattoo of a large red rose on the right thigh. The painted-on pubic hair is green instead of black. The toenails are long and pointed.

The legs are also coated in a white oily cream that smells of candle wax. It's the same odor that coated the upstairs bedroom. Now I know where it came from—it's some kind of Matryoshkan bodily fluid. The stuff must be everywhere in the sanctuary, covering all the furniture like jism in a seedy hotel room.

"You'll see me when it's over," Ynaria tells me.

Then she pulls off the top half of her body and drops it to the floor like a wet pile of laundry. The sight makes me weak in the knees. Seeing her outer layer lying on the floor like that hits me with such shock I have to prop myself up with the back of a chair. It's like she's dead, a lifeless husk discarded on the ground.

What remains is a completely new, yet slightly smaller, woman covered in milky goo. Her short green hair is wetted down flat to her head. Her dark blue eyes stare at me as she takes deep, long breaths. We just stare at each other for a while. I don't really know what to say. She licks her skinny, colorless lips and steps forward.

"Hi, Benny," she says.

Her voice is completely different from Ynaria's. It's deeper, yet more youthful, like the voice of a teenager.

"I'm Vera."

When she says her name, I twitch in distress. I didn't realize I'd be meeting the crazy one so soon. I thought she'd be deeper in.

Before I can say anything, she lunges at me, wraps

her arms around me and presses herself tightly against my body, covering me in her weird inner mucus.

"I've wanted to hold you in my own arms for so long," she says. "It feels amazing."

I hug her back. She is part of Ynaria, after all. I shouldn't be scared of her. While holding her against me, I notice that her skin is much softer than Ynaria's. Her flesh is like that of a human's. In fact, everything about her is more human than Ynaria. The warmth and texture of her skin, the fuzziness of her hair, the softness of her lips when she kisses my chin. She doesn't even have Ynaria's glowing circles on her cheeks.

Then she backs up and looks me in the eyes.

"Don't be weirded out," she says. "You're going to love me. I promise."

Vera goes upstairs to shower the fluids off of her, leaving me alone with Ynaria's husk on the floor.

I go to what is left of Ynaria, examining her deflated remains. I'm taken aback when I notice her breathing. The husk is still alive. I reach out and touch it. Her skin pulses, wiggles like my fingers are tickling her. But the inside of her is hollow. When I look inside, all I see is the white fluid and fleshy tissue. There are no organs or blood vessels that I can see. I don't know what's keeping her alive.

"This trial is one-sided," Vera says, coming down the stairs in a yellow t-shirt and shorts. The clothes are brand new. Ynaria must have bought them just for this occasion. "It's not fair."

She stands in front of me, drying her hair with a white towel. Her hair is fluffier and a much brighter shade of green than I originally thought it was. It must have looked dark when she first came out of her shell because it was still wet. I wonder if it's naturally green or if she dyes it. Judging by her pubic hair and eyebrows, it's most likely natural. I've never seen a Matryoshkan with natural green hair before. I didn't realize an inner layer would be so different.

"Why's that?" I ask.

"Because you get to see inside of me, but I don't get to see inside of you," she says. "It kind of makes me want to cut you open to see what you look like underneath your skin."

As I slowly back away, Vera bursts into laughter.

"I'm just fucking with you," she says. "I knew that would freak you out."

I put on a smile. "Yeah, it kind of freaked me out."

"Relax." She tosses the wet towel on the table. "Even though we're different people, I'm still your fiancé. Every moment you spent with Ynaria, you also spent with me. Every time we made love, you made love to me. Every feeling she ever felt for you, I felt it too. We are the same person with the same memories. We just have different minds, different personalities."

"Yeah, I know," I say.

She points at Ynaria's husk. "Think of her as makeup and fancy clothing. I'm who she is at the end of the day, when the makeup and outfit comes off. I'm her comfy clothes."

"I see," I tell her, then I point at her outfit. "You even wear more comfortable clothes. I've never seen Ynaria wear shorts before."

She looks down and smirks. "Yeah, I don't do dresses. I hope that's okay with you."

"No, it's fine," I say.

She grabs the champagne and drinks right from the bottle.

"How long will you be Vera?" I ask.

She puts on a fake sneer. "What? Are you trying to get rid of me already?"

I shake my head. "No, I'm just curious."

She takes another swig from the bottle. "Depends. It could be hours. It could be days."

"Why's that?" I ask.

She says, "I won't open up to reveal the next layer until I'm convinced that you love me just as much as you love Ynaria."

"Really?" I ask. "That could take a *long* time."

She spits champagne onto the floor and bursts into laughter. "Oh, you think that much of me, do you?"

Her laughter makes me chuckle as well, realizing how offensive my words must have sounded.

"No, that's not what I meant," I say. "It takes a long time to get to know somebody, let alone fall in love with them. It took me months before I fell completely in love with Ynaria. We're not going to be here for months, are we?"

Vera smiles and comes to me. "You won't need that long."

Then she wraps her arms around me. She feels so different from Ynaria, yet comfortable and familiar. It really is like I'm hugging Ynaria if her mind was transported into a more petite body.

"You already love me." She kisses me on the chin in the way Ynaria always does. "You just don't realize it yet."

She separates from me and gazes deep into my eyes with a stern expression.

"Unless your love for Ynaria only goes skin-deep," she says.

I shake my head. "It's not just skin-deep. I will love all of her. I promise."

She smirks. "We'll see about that."

Vera looks down at Ynaria's husk and says, "Help me move her into the next room. She's too distracting. I don't want her to spoil our time together."

I just nod in agreement. We pick up Ynaria's wet husk and move it into a large storage room that resembles a morgue. There are large metal drawers in the wall, each one big enough to hold a corpse. We place Ynaria into the first one, closest to the floor. Then slide it shut.

As we leave the room and close the door, I ask, "How

long can she live separated from the rest of you?"

"A couple months," she says. "But it's unhealthy to go for more than a few weeks, for her and the rest of us. We'd wither and grow sick."

We sit down on the living room couch.

"What's the longest you've gone outside of her body?" I ask.

"Five days," she says, inching herself closer to me.

"Really, that long?" I ask.

She nods. "Ynaria was really depressed after her last boyfriend left her for a human girl. She couldn't take it anymore, so she shut down. For three months, all she did was go to work and left me in control for the rest of the time. I had the run of the place." She smiles like it was a good memory. "At one point, she called in sick and gave me a five day weekend. Bad idea. You can say that when Ynaria gets depressed, *I* get angry. I tore apart her apartment, burning everything that reminded me of that asshole. I would have beat the shit out of him if I saw him. I fantasized about breaking into his apartment and cutting something off. I'm not sure what I would have cut off. His ear, his dick. I just wanted to cut off *something*, even if it was just his stupid mustache."

"You didn't, I'm guessing?" I ask.

She shakes her head, fluffing her green hair at me. "Nah, I don't like leaving the house without Ynaria on. I'm more of a homebody. Going outside for me would be like going outside naked for you."

I nod. I'm not sure I understand how that feels, but

I get the analogy.

"Have you ever gone out in public?" I ask.

She smiles and nods. "A few times, but not for long. It felt like I was streaking. Usually I'd just go for quick two-minute sprints around the neighborhood just to see if I was brave enough to do it. But there was one time I went out for hours."

"What did you do?" I ask.

She lifts up the side of her shorts to expose the large tattoo covering the majority of her right thigh. "I got a tattoo."

"Seriously?" I ask.

I find myself reaching out to touch the tattoo. Vera holds my hand against my leg as I feel her, like she doesn't want me to let her go.

"I always wanted a tattoo, but my parents would kill me if they knew I got one," she says. "That's why I did it instead of Ynaria. I could have a tattoo and nobody would ever know. *You* didn't even know."

I shake my head. "I had no idea."

She smiles. "Then it's our secret. Don't ever tell my parents."

I nod.

"You said Ynaria was depressed after her last boyfriend left her," I say. "She never told me about him. What was he like?"

"Well, he was human, like you," she says.

"Really? I didn't know she dated a human besides me."

Vera slaps me on the shoulder. "Watch your pronouns.

It hurts my feelings."

I have no idea what she's talking about until I think over what I just said.

"I'm sorry," I say, then I correct myself. "I didn't know *you* dated a human besides me."

"That's better." She smiles. "Anyway, yeah. His name was Terry. I was head over heels in love with the guy. But he left me for a human girl, said he was just experimenting with me and couldn't take a relationship with a *nesting doll* seriously."

"What a prick," I say.

She slaps me again, but this time with approval. "I know, right? He treated me like I wasn't even a real person. It was demeaning." Vera inches closer to me on the couch and rests her shoulder against mine. "I swore off human guys after that, thought they were all that way. But then I met you. You made me change my mind about human guys. You're not *all* pricks."

"Thanks," I say.

She squeezes me against her. "I'm glad you proved me wrong."

We get hungry and look through the cabinets to see what the church left for us.

"There's enough food here to last for months," I say.

Vera nods. "Yeah, they really hooked us up. Everyone at the church contributed."

She pulls out spaghetti noodles and sauce. "I'll cook tonight. You cook tomorrow."

"Sure," I say.

While she tears open the package of spaghetti with her teeth, spilling noodles across the kitchen counter, I just study the woman, trying to imagine her having lived inside of Ynaria all this time. It's still hard to believe. I never expected her to be so different.

Vera hocks up a loogie into her mouth and spits it toward the sink. It misses and hits the side of the counter, then rolls off onto the floor. She gets tomato sauce all over her when she opens the jar, but doesn't bother cleaning it up. She just wipes her hand on the back of her yellow shorts, leaving a large red handprint on her butt. Part of me is beginning to realize that Vera is the slobby *doesn't-give-a-shit* side of Ynaria.

"Grate the cheese," Vera tells me when she sees me just standing around.

"Sure," I say.

I open the fridge. There's so much food and it's so neatly packed. The people from the church did a very efficient job, organizing it like a grocery store shelf. While going through the cheese drawer, I realize that there are no Italian-style cheeses. It's all Matryoshkan styles, which I can't really tell apart. I just grab whatever looks most similar to parmesan.

Vera peeks over my shoulder and sees a container of meat on the top shelf.

"Oh, give me that," she says, pointing.

I pick up the package. "What is it?"

"Rabbit," she says. "I love rabbit."

"Rabbit?" I say in a soft voice. I look at the package. The rabbit is skinned and gutted, but the whole body is in there, head and everything.

She notices the sad look on my face.

"Don't like rabbits?" she asks.

"I love rabbits… as pets," I say. "I had a bunny named Snuffy when I was a little kid."

"You had a pet rabbit?" She laughs. "That's so weird."

She takes the package and rips it open with her fingernails.

"It's a pretty common pet," I say.

"If I had a pet rabbit I would have been too tempted to eat it," she says. "Rabbit was my favorite food as a kid."

"You'd eat your own pet? But bunnies are so cute."

She giggles. "I know! That's what makes them taste so good."

Then she chops the head off of the rabbit carcass with a white butcher knife.

Sitting at the dinner table, I sip on a glass of red wine, eating the spaghetti with careful bites. The rabbit parts poke out from under the cheese, the meat still on the bone. The flavor of rabbit doesn't mix well with the marinara sauce, giving it a bloody, gamey taste. It's also much creamier than I would have expected, like Vera added milk to the sauce. But I think it's just from the cheese. Matryoshkan cheese always tastes milky when it's melted.

"So what do you think so far?" she asks, sitting across from me, her fingers coated in marinara sauce as she eats the rabbit with her fingers.

"It's good," I say, lying through my teeth.

I look down at the rabbit head on my plate as it stares up at me with hollow sockets. Vera gave me the head just to freak me out. She said the brain is the best part, but I'm pretty sure she just wants to see if she can get me to eat it.

I add, "Thanks for making it."

She shakes her head. "Not the food. I'm talking about *me*. What do you think of me so far?"

Then she rubs my knees with her bare feet beneath the table. I cough as her toes curl around the fabric of my pants.

I smile at her. "You're great."

"Tell me everything you like about me so far," she says, leaning forward. "Compare me to Ynaria."

"Well…" I try to think. I hate being put on the spot.

"Don't think about it," she says. "Just tell me the first thing on your mind. Be honest."

"Your hair," I say, rubbing my own head. "I love your green hair."

She smiles and fluffs her hair. "Really? Better than Ynaria's?"

I blush and say, "Yeah, kind of."

But I really regret saying this after the words come out. It feels like a betrayal. Will Ynaria be jealous that

I said I like Vera's hair better than hers? Or does it matter? Maybe it's like telling a girl you like her hair better when it's up than when it's down. Maybe it doesn't matter.

She smiles brighter, as though excited to hear me admit this. "You do?"

I backtrack a little. "Well, I really love Ynaria's hair, but green is one of my favorite colors. I love that you have natural green hair."

She rubs her hair with both hands, not concerned with the spaghetti sauce on her fingers.

"It's also softer," I say. "It's even softer than a human's. And I've always liked girls with short hair for some reason. It's really cute."

"Ynaria doesn't have short hair." She says this almost proudly, like it's an accomplishment to have better hair than her outer layer.

"Ynaria's hair looks good long," I say. "Your hair looks good short."

She nods. "That's good, because it doesn't grow any longer than this. I've tried. It doesn't work." She picks sauce out of strands of her hair. "The curse of being an inner layer." She wipes her hands on a handful of bunched-up pre-used napkins, one finger at a time. "What else do you like about me?"

"Well, you're really open," I say. "You seem down-to-earth. Easier to talk to I guess. Not shy at all."

"I'm like Ynaria when she's drunk," she says, chewing rabbit meat as she speaks.

I smile. "Yeah, a little bit."

She pushes her foot higher up my leg so that she can rest her heel on my thigh.

"You're also a lot more touchy-feely," I say. "More affectionate."

She nods. "I don't *feel* much when I'm inside Ynaria, so I like using my sense of touch as much as possible when I get out. My skin is more sensitive. Everything feels good." She wiggles her toes against me. "*You* feel good."

Then she smiles.

"So far, you seem… comfortable," I say. "That's what I like best about you. I feel like I can say or do anything around you and you wouldn't care."

"Don't fart around me," she says.

Her words catch me off guard. "What?"

"I hate the smell of human farts," she says. "*Ewww.* They're so gross. Just saying…"

"Okay, I guess I'll try not to fart around you," I say.

"Humans are fart machines," she says. "I hate that."

I just nod, not sure why she's bringing up farting. Nesting doll farts aren't any better. They smell like dirty laundry.

"You haven't said I'm pretty yet," she says.

"Huh?" I ask, still thinking about the fart comment.

"Don't you think I'm pretty?" she asks with spaghetti sauce matted into her hair.

I look at her. Her facial features are so much different than Ynaria's. More narrow. Higher cheekbones. Small pointed nose. Skinny eyebrows. More slender of a neck.

"Yes," I say. "I think you're very pretty."

Though there's no other answer to that question, I meant what I said. She's really attractive. In fact, I don't think I've ever seen a prettier nesting doll girl.

"Even prettier than Ynaria?" she asks.

I don't know how to respond to that one. I just stare at her, thinking of my response.

She smiles. "You can say I'm prettier than Ynaria if you want. She won't be offended, if that's what you're worried about. I'd be flattered if you were more attracted to my inner layers than you are to me. It means a lot if you'd find my insides even more beautiful than my outside."

"In some ways, yes," I tell her. "You are definitely prettier."

"Hell yeah I am!" She laughs out loud and raises her fists in triumph. "Ynaria's going to be so pissed!"

My mouth drops open. "What? I thought you said she wouldn't be offended?"

"I totally lied!" She slams her hand on the table. "She thinks she's so much prettier. She's going to be so jealous."

"You tricked me," I say.

She keeps laughing and pointing at me. "And you better not think any of the other layers are prettier than me. I'll kick your ass if you think they're prettier than me. I want to be the prettiest."

"I said in *some* ways you're prettier than Ynaria," I say. "I didn't say you were the prettiest."

"Too late," she says. "I'm not buying it. You like me best."

I just shake my head at her. Part of me thinks she's just fucking with me and Ynaria won't care at all. Another part of me is really worried about what will happen once she's put back together at the end of The Trial.

"It's a good thing, too," she says. "You'll probably be seeing a lot of me once we're married. I don't like wearing Ynaria when I'm lying around the house. We'll be spending whole weekends watching movies in bed together."

After dinner, we take a new bottle of wine and go upstairs to the bedroom. She presses herself against me and kisses me deeper than Ynaria ever has before. She's so much more passionate than Ynaria, so much more aggressive. It's hard to think that she's really a part of my fiancé and not a completely different person. As I kiss her, it feels like I'm cheating with another woman.

She pulls off her shirt and pulls my hand to her breast. It's much smaller than Ynaria's, but softer, more human. When I close my eyes, she doesn't seem like a nesting doll at all.

We have the best sex I've ever had in my life. She's animalistic in bed. Jumping on top of me, clawing at my hair. Ynaria moans quietly when we make love, but Vera screams at the top of her lungs like she wants everyone in the world to hear her. And she's not afraid to tell me what she wants me to do. She tells me to bite her nipples, lick her neck. She tells me to give her oral sex, pushing my face down to her flat green pubic region.

Everything about it is better than it's been with Ynaria. Vera is so unrestrained, so open. I had no idea there was someone like her inside of Ynaria all this time.

When we finish, we collapse against the mattress and breathe deep, exhausted breaths.

"Holy shit…" Vera says. "I loved that so much."

I'm still in shock, still shaking. "Yeah…"

Then she laughs and rolls over onto me. "I've never had sex outside of Ynaria before. It's *so* much better."

I find myself nodding in agreement.

"Let's do this all the time when we're married," she says. "I'm way more into it than Ynaria is."

"As long as she doesn't get jealous…" I say.

She giggles. "She's had you long enough. *I'm* the one who should be jealous."

Vera curls around me and goes to sleep almost instantly, the bright iridescent lights still shining down on us. It takes a while to fall asleep, still in shock from how good the sex was, still mystified from the whole experience of meeting the girl living inside my fiancé. Within an hour, Vera is snoring loudly into my neck. A large puddle of drool forms on my chest. And even though it's horribly uncomfortable, I wouldn't want to be anywhere else in the world.

The next morning, I find Vera downstairs, walking around the kitchen without any clothes on, cleaning up the mess we left behind the night before.

"Good, you're up," she says. "I was just about to wake you."

She comes to me and sucks my tongue into her mouth, not even caring about my morning breath. Her arms squeeze tightly against my back. When her lips part from mine, she rests her forehead against my neck. Her soft green hair tickles my nose.

"I'm going to open up now," she says. "I want you to meet my next layer."

I step back and look her in the eyes. "Already?"

"Yeah, I think it's time," she says.

"But it's only been a day," I say. "We can spend another day together. Just one more day."

"We'll have our whole lives together once we're married," she says.

"But I thought you said you wouldn't change until you were certain that I've fallen in love with you."

She laughs. "But you have fallen in love with me."

"How do you know?"

She smiles and kisses my cheek. Then she whispers in my ear, "Because you don't want me to go."

I laugh and nod at her. She's got a good point. I'd love to spend the whole week with just her.

"But what if I don't like the others as much as I like you?" I ask.

She shakes her head. "You won't. I'm the best one. Get used to it."

"Are you ready?" she asks.

I nod.

She strokes the crease in her middle until it moistens with fluid. As she curls her fingers inside of her flesh, I wonder what the next layer will be like. I wonder if she will be as weird and cute as Vera. I wonder if she will be even better. It would be just like Ynaria if every layer was even better than the last. That's the kind of woman she is. She never ceases to amaze me.

Then Vera takes her body off.

When I see the person step out of Vera's empty husk, I have to do a double-take, not able to believe my own eyes. The new figure is not a beautiful woman like Vera. It's not even a woman at all. It's a man—a short, bearded man with bright red hair.

"Hey, Ben!" the guy says, wiping the milky fluid from his chest. "What's up, bro? It's so good to finally meet you. I'm Pavel."

Then he comes up to me and gives me a big bear hug.

CHAPTER THREE
PAVEL

I was expecting to be surprised by some of Ynaria's inner layers, but I never expected any of them would be male.

Pavel puts on a white pocket t-shirt and tucks it into a pair of blue jeans. He straightens his cherry-red hair with a switchblade comb from the 1980s and then stores it in his back pocket. He's about the same size I was when I was a junior high student, only he doesn't look like a kid. He's just a very petite adult male, small enough to fit inside of Vera.

"We're going to have so much fun, bro," he says. "I've been waiting forever to hang out with you. It'll be sweet."

I don't say a word to him, just staring. Unlike Vera, this guy doesn't seem anything like Ynaria whatsoever. He just seems like some random guy who broke into the sanctuary when I wasn't looking.

"You want to get a beer?" he asks. "Let's drink some beer."

I don't accept the offer, but he heads for the kitchen anyway. I decide not to follow. Instead, I take Vera's husk to the back room and store it in the drawer above Ynaria's. With Vera, I was expecting someone crazy and horrible but ended up being pleasantly surprised. Now she's just an empty suit of flesh that quivers and sweats against my arms. I try not to look down at her as I put her in storage. Her face looks so disturbing in its deflated state that it's likely to give me nightmares.

When I get back, Pavel is opening two bottles of Matryoshkan lager using only his teeth.

"Think fast," he says, tossing me an open bottle.

I catch it just before it hits the floor, but half the beer foams out over my hands. Pavel takes a long drink of his beer, staring at me as he does it as though he wants to prove he can drink faster than I can. I don't attempt to compete.

"So…" I begin. I'm not sure what else to say to him except the obvious. "You're a guy…"

He laughs. "Yeah, looks like it."

I take a sip of beer foam. "I didn't know one of Ynaria's inner layers was male. I didn't even know that was possible."

He shrugs. "It's pretty common for Matryoshkans to contain a variety of genders. Everyone has a masculine side and a feminine side. You can say I'm Ynaria's masculine side."

"Are any more of you male?" I ask.

He shakes his head. "Just me."

"And I'm supposed to fall in love with you as well?" I ask.

He smirks. "We don't have to fuck if that's what

you're worried about. I know you're not attracted to dudes."

I shake my head. "That's not what I meant."

"You can if you want." He grabs his dick through his pants. "I've never used this thing for anything but jerking off. I'd love to fuck you with it."

I cringe and step away. "No, thank you. I'm good."

"Are you sure?" he asks. "It's not really gay. I'm still Ynaria, you know. Just think of her as dressed up like a guy, wearing a very realistic strap-on dildo."

I shake my head. "Sorry, I don't think that's going to happen. I don't want to have sex with a man."

He laughs and takes another swig.

"Well, actually…" he says, a weird smile curls on the side of his lips. "You do know that you've already been fucking me every time you made love to Ynaria, don't you? When you have sex with us, your dick goes into all of our vaginas at once."

"Seriously?" I ask. "But you don't have a vagina."

"Actually, I have both," he says. He goes to pull down his pants. "I'll show you."

I hold up my hands. "No. Thanks. I believe you."

He re-buttons his jeans. "Don't get weirded out by it. I don't want to lose you just because I'm male. That's why I never mentioned it before. I figured you'd be this way."

I nod. "It's going to take some getting used to."

He comes to me and puts his arm around my waist. "Look, it's cool, bro. I don't need you to love me in that way. I just want you to get to know me. I'm sure you'll like me in no time."

"So it's cool if we don't have sex?" I ask. "Ever?"

He nods and smiles. "Oh, yeah. Totally cool if we just hang out together."

"Okay, sounds good," I say. "Let's hang."

We clink our beer bottles together and take a swig.

Three beers later:

"Why the fuck won't you sleep with me?" Pavel cries, lying on the couch with a beer tucked under his armpit. "You slept with Vera. You should sleep with me, too."

"You said it would be cool if we didn't have sex," I argue, wondering how the hell he changed his mind so fast.

"Yeah, but I was just trying to be nice," he says, slurring his words. "I thought you'd change your mind. If you really loved me, you'd change your mind."

"Dude, you're drunk," I say. "How'd you get drunk so quickly?"

He shakes his head. "I'm small. I don't need that much."

I try to keep his mind off of sex. "We should play a game or something. Are there board games here?"

"Nah." He sits up. "I *thought* about bringing one. We can't have television, but board games are okay. I just don't have any at home and didn't get around to buying any."

"We can play cards," I say.

"You brought cards?"

"No, but I brought pens and paper. We can make cards."

"You can what..." Pavel seems amazed by the idea of making your own cards, as though he never would have thought of doing that in a million years.

I go to my backpack and pull out a pad of paper and pens. We tear up the paper into small squares and write numbers with suits on them. When we have a full deck, I go into the kitchen and grab some snack items to use as chips.

"What are we playing?" Pavel asks, trying to shuffle the deck.

"Poker, of course," I tell him. Then I point at the food I brought out to the table. "The pretzels are one dollar bills, the chocolates are five dollar bills, and these weird dick-shaped shortbread cookies are ten dollar bills."

After I say this, I realize I probably shouldn't have chosen anything that looks penis-like for our poker chips, or at least I shouldn't have described them that way. They aren't even all that dick-shaped. I think they are supposed to be rowboats or something.

Pavel smiles. "I'm going to win all of the dicks you've got."

I just shake my head, not wanting to acknowledge his comment.

"You know how to play Texas Hold'em?" I ask.

He nods. "The only way to play."

I agree, though I'm surprised to hear him say this. I had no idea Ynaria played poker, let alone Hold'em poker.

"Though strip poker would be even better," he says.

I shake my head. "No strip poker."

"You're no fun," he says.

But it doesn't bother me. I'm perfectly fine with being no fun in this case.

Heads up poker isn't as enjoyable as playing with a large group of people, but Pavel keeps it entertaining. He's actually pretty good, maybe better than me. I can never tell when he's bluffing. But I like the challenge. It's no fun to play a game of strategy like poker without a skilled opponent. I'm learning more about Ynaria than I expected I would just by playing a game of cards.

"Pocket aces," Pavel says, revealing his hand. He smiles as he takes the pot again. "You're losing, Benny."

"It's not over yet," I say.

He takes a big chug of his beer, getting drunker by the minute.

"If you don't beat me I'll never respect you," he says.

"I'll beat you. I'm just getting warmed up."

With the next hand, I go in hard. That's the trick to heads up poker. Neither of you are likely to have great cards, so if you have anything at all it's most likely better than your opponent's.

As we play, I ask Pavel a question. It's something I've been thinking about all week. Something Ynaria's father said to me.

"So the other night..." I say. "At the dinner with your family, your father said that you become other people as you get older. What's that all about?"

Pavel leaves my question hanging as he thinks about his next move. Once he makes a decision, he raises me three pretzels and says, "Yeah, Ynaria won't always be the outer layer. If I live long enough I'll grow up to three new layers. It's kind of like the reverse of a snake shedding its skin. We grow extra layers of skin with age. One day, Ynaria will become just another inner layer, like me and Vera."

This idea is frightening to me. I can't believe I won't be able to spend my whole life with Ynaria. At some point, I'll be spending my life with somebody completely new. Someone like Pavel or Vera. Someone who might be nothing like the woman I married.

I raise him a dick cookie and ask, "Seriously?"

He nods. Then he reaches out and rests his hand on my shoulder, trying to comfort me. He can tell I'm a little distressed over the idea.

"Not for a long time," he says. "Don't worry. The next layer won't grow until I'm at least forty. By marrying young, you'll have plenty of time before the next change."

"Will I still be able to see Ynaria whenever I want?" I ask. "Even when she's an inner layer?"

"Of course," he says. Then he calls my bet. "You'll be

able to see me whenever you want as well. But, remember, when you're with the outer layer, you're with all of us. That won't ever change. You'll have to come to terms with the fact that we're all the same person. When you're with one of us, you're with all of us, always."

"Does the outer layer know what's happening when she's taken off?"

Pavel shakes his head. "No, Ynaria won't experience anything we do together while she's in the box. But once I put her back on, and our minds are linked together, she'll be filled in on everything she missed. She won't exactly share the memories, but she'll know everything that occurred. There's nothing I'm able to hide from her once we're combined into one person."

I nod. Then I ask, "Will any of your new layers be male, like you?"

He shrugs. "Maybe. You never know until it happens."

I nod. I can probably deal with Ynaria becoming a new person one day, but I don't think I can handle if she turns male. One male layer is enough.

"So are you going to play or what?" Pavel asks.

I raise him three chocolates and he folds. He only had a pair of eights.

"I'm gaining on you," I tell him.

"It won't last," he responds.

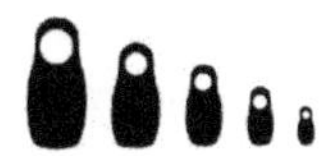

After the game, Pavel is pissed that I beat him. He

thought he had me until the third to last hand, where we both went all in on a hand where he thought for sure that his three of a kind was going to beat my flush. But my win doesn't feel right. Pavel has gotten so drunk that he started making poor decisions. He probably would have beaten me if he was sober.

"This sucks," he says, throwing his paper cards down with drunken rage. "I was so going to force you to let me fuck you if you lost."

I shake my head. "Good thing you got too drunk to win."

His red eyebrows curl in annoyance, "What do you mean it's a *good thing?* You act like the idea of me fucking you is disgusting?"

"I'm not into guys," I say. "I'm sorry."

"You don't know what you're missing," he says, slurring his words. "It could be magical."

I just linger in silence for a while, not wanting to continue the conversation. But he keeps staring at me, waiting for me to say something. He's not going to let it go.

I tell him, "When you're Ynaria, it's magical. When you're Vera, it's definitely magical. But you're a guy. The idea of having sex with a guy is just not something that appeals to me whatsoever. To be honest, I think it's disturbing."

He's offended by my choice of words. He finishes his beer and gets a new one from the refrigerator and puts it down on the table.

"But I'm still *me*," he says. "I just look different. I

think it's really selfish and shallow of you to turn me down just because you're not attracted to men."

With his slurred speech, I can tell it's just the alcohol talking. I don't respond to him. I just stand up and take his unopened beer from the table, then put it back in the fridge.

"Look..." He sits up, trying to sober up in order to reason with me. "I'm not upset you don't want to do it. I'm upset that you won't even try it. Who knows, you might like it."

I sit down in a chair across from him. "I know I won't like it."

He argues, "If you had an inner layer that was female, I'd totally have lesbian sex with you as Vera or Ynaria. Why won't you have gay sex with me?"

I just groan at him. I'm beginning to understand what it must have been like for Ynaria all those nights when we first started dating, when I was horny and relentless with her. Men are kind of pathetic when they want to have sex with you.

"It's not happening," I say.

"Well, I'm cancelling The Trial unless you do," he says.

"What?" I yell. "You're seriously going go threaten me with that?"

"If that's what it takes," he says.

"Can't we just hang out?" I ask. "Let's play another round of poker."

I start shuffling the cards, but Pavel knocks them out of my hands.

"I've never had sex with my penis before," he says. "Don't you know how frustrating that is?"

"I'll buy a prostitute for you some day if you want," I tell him. "I promise."

His eyebrows curl in anger. "What? Are you fucking serious? I don't want a prostitute, I want you. I can't believe you'd have me sleep with somebody else." He looks away and shakes his head. "Fucking asshole."

"Why am I an asshole? If Ynaria got really fat or grew a beard I wouldn't want to have sex with her either."

His mouth widens in shock. "You wouldn't have sex with me just because I got fat? You're such an asshole."

I forget for a second that I'm talking to Ynaria and not some other guy. I say, "That's not what I meant. I just mean that you can't expect me to want to sleep with you if I don't find you sexually desirable."

Tears fall from his eyes. "I can't believe you…"

"I'm sorry. I just don't want to have sex with you while you're male."

He shakes his head, wiping his tears away. "Forget it. If you don't want to make love to me then this trial is over."

"What?" I ask, raising my voice.

"You obviously don't love me."

"That's not true," I say.

"If you loved me you would see past the fact that I'm a guy."

"But I'm not gay!"

He shrugs. "It shouldn't matter."

"But it matters to me."

He shakes his head. "This isn't going to work. If you're not even going to try it then you're not the person I thought you were. I can't imagine spending the rest of my life with you."

Pavel puts his face in a couch cushion to hold back the tears. He doesn't look at me. He just sobs and pouts, buried in the pillow. I try to apologize, but he won't listen to a word I say.

I sigh and find myself saying, "Fine, I'll do it."

I can't believe I said that. Pavel can't believe it either. I wonder if it's possible to take back my words.

"Wait…" he says, his tears disappear in an instant. "Seriously?"

I think about it for a moment, then I close my eyes and nod at him.

"I love Ynaria," I say. "I'll do anything for her. If this is what I have to do in order to pass The Trial, then I'll do it."

He jumps up from the couch with excitement. It's as though he never was upset in the first place, like all of it was an act this whole time in order to guilt me into agreement.

"That's the spirit, bro!" he says.

He holds out his hand to lift me out of my seat.

I frown at him. "But I'm not going to like it."

He smiles. "I'm totally cool with that."

"And this is the one and only time," I say.

He nods. "Sure. Whatever. I just want to see what it feels like to put *my* dick in *you* for a change."

I cringe at the thought.

When I get to my feet, I say, "Actually, I'm going to have to chug some more beer first."

"No problem," he says. "Just chug them quickly. I'm ready to go."

When he points at the erection in his pants, I realize I'll never be able to tell Rick or Mark about the Pavel layer of Ynaria. Not ever.

After it's over, I lie on the bed, staring at the ceiling, somewhat traumatized by the whole experience. It was even worse than I imagined. I've never felt dirtier.

Pavel, on the other hand, couldn't be more pleased with himself. He lies next to me with a big smile on his face.

"That was so cool," he says. "Having a dick is awesome."

That would be a weird thing to say if he wasn't usually a woman. He doesn't remind me much of Ynaria, but he does have some resemblance to Vera. If Vera had a penis that's exactly what she would say.

"Yeah..." I respond.

"Man, I could go for a cheeseburger," Pavel says. "Doesn't a cheeseburger sound good right about now?"

It's an odd request. Matryoshkans don't normally eat cheeseburgers or any kind of sandwich-like food.

"Do we have cheeseburgers?" I ask.

He thinks about it. Then he says, "No. It would be good though, wouldn't it?"

I nod.

"Or a cheeseburger omelet. I love ground beef in eggs."

"You do?" I ask. "I've never seen Ynaria eat that before."

"Well, I have a different tongue than her," he says. "We like different things."

"Really?"

"She's a picky eater. She has to eat food that agrees with all of our palettes."

I nod, but not quite sure I understand.

A thick fluid leaks down my thigh and I realize I need to clean up. Immediately.

"I'm going to take a shower," I tell him, getting up from the bed.

"Cool," he says. "I'll join you in a few minutes."

"No, that's okay," I say. "You can stay here."

"Cool," he says, pulling the covers up to his neck.

In the bathroom, I turn on the water so hot that it burns the memory of what just happened right out of my brain.

When I get back, I put on new clothes from the dresser. The most comfortable clothes I can find.

Pavel comes to me, naked, and puts his hand on my shoulder.

"What?" I ask.

"I'm going to reveal the next layer now," he says.

"Really?" I ask. "I thought I needed to fall in love

with you before you'd do that."

He laughs. "Dude, you're straight and you let me fuck you anyway. If that's not true love then I don't know what it is."

"I only did it because you wouldn't shut up about it," I say.

"Don't ruin it, bro," he says with a smile. "I know you love me."

Then he winks at me.

I shake my head at him.

"Until next time," he says.

Then he pulls off his legs. Beneath him, six blue tentacles ooze across the tile floor. He sees the look of shock growing on my face.

"Oh, word of warning," he says, glancing down at his tentacle legs. "My layers get a little weird from here on out. Try not to freak out."

CHAPTER FOUR
EKATERINA

Ynaria's fourth layer is like nothing I expected. She's not even human. The blue figure pushes Pavel's upper body off of her, revealing a small woman with deep black fishy eyes and long purple tentacles instead of hair. Her skin is a mixture of scales and human-like flesh. The lower half of her body is that of an octopus. She's not human, she's not even nesting doll. She's like some kind of alien creature.

"I'm Ekaterina," she says, her voice high and gurgling like her throat is filled with fluid.

The room fills with a pungent fish-like odor. I can't help but cover my nose as she slithers across the floor toward me.

"Hold me," she says, wrapping her wet arms around my body.

The odor is so strong that I start dry-heaving into my mouth, but I hug her anyway. She rests her head on my stomach, her tentacle hair curls around my waist. She smells like death, like a barrel of dead squid. I can't breathe in the stench for another second and have to push her away from me.

When she sees me dry-heaving behind the bed, she stares at me in horror. Her wide eyes quiver. Tears form on her cheeks. Then she starts to bawl.

"Waaaa!" she screams. "You don't like me!"

I hold up my hand, trying to be polite. "No, it's not that. I'm just a little sensitive to the smell."

When she hears my words, she cries even louder. "You don't like my smell! Waaaa!"

"I'm sure it will be fine," I say. Then a fountain of beer splashes up my throat and geysers to the floor.

"You think I'm gross!" she cries, slithering back.

Her tentacle hair curls around her face in embarrassment.

"I don't think you're gross," I say.

She hiccups between sobs, shaking her head, burying her face in her scaly hands.

"You're disgusted by me!"

"I'm not disgusted." I hold out my hands to her, but keep my distance from her smell. "I'm just surprised. I didn't know any of your layers looked so… *different*."

She sobs into her hands. "You think I'm weird!"

Ekaterina is incredibly sensitive. I realize I have to choose my words very carefully around her. Who knows what will set her off.

I say, "So what. There's nothing wrong with weird. I like weird."

She peeks up from her tentacles, widening her black pool eyes.

"Really?" she asks.

"Yeah," I say, scratching the back of my neck. "Your

tentacles, your skin color, your eyes.... They make you look unique. Nobody on Earth looks like you do."

She wipes her tears away. "So you think I'm pretty?"

I hesitate to respond right away. I look at her slithering figure, trying to find some part of her to compliment. She has no breasts, no curves, no feminine elements whatsoever. The only thing remotely attractive about her is her face. She has a flat nose, big bulging eyes, and thick purple fish lips, but there's something cute about it, like a cute alien cartoon character.

I say, "Yeah, I think you're cute."

"Really?" She smiles widely. "Do you think I'm prettier than Vera and Ynaria?"

"Well..." I pause to think about whether I should lie or not, but dishonesty probably would not go over very well in the long term. I decide to tell the truth. "Not as pretty as Vera or Ynaria, but I still think you're cute."

Slightly cute is more accurate, but I don't want to be *that* honest.

But my response is still not good enough. Ekaterina drops her mouth open and bawls at the top of her lungs.

"You think I'm ugly!" she cries.

"What? I said you were cute."

"You hate me!"

"I don't hate you!"

Then she races into the bathroom and slams the door.

It's been hours and Ekaterina won't leave the bathroom. She just cries, alternating between gentle sobs and wailing screams. She's kind of a psychopath.

"Come on, Ekaterina," I say through the bathroom door. "Come out."

I'm not sure I actually want her to come out, but I don't know what else to do. On one hand, I'm glad I don't have to look at her or deal with her stink. But on the other, we won't be able to continue with The Trial if she refuses to face me.

"No," she says. "You don't love me. You're *never* going to love me."

"How do you know?" I ask. "We've hardly spent any time together."

"I make you throw up!" she cries.

"That's just because I drank too much beer on an empty stomach," I say. "Don't take it personally."

She ignores my comment and says, "My father did this on purpose! He knew you'd hate me if you met me! He knew you'd leave me once you got to my layer!"

I shake my head. "I'm not going to leave you."

"He doesn't want us to get married!" she cries. "He tricked us! We never should have done The Trial at all!"

"I'm not giving up," I say. "I still want to marry you."

But she doesn't listen to a single word I say.

"Nobody will ever marry me!"

Then she cries and kicks at the door with her tentacle legs.

"Just come out," I say. "You haven't eaten anything all day. At least have some dinner."

But she doesn't respond. She just cries louder and louder until I leave the room and head downstairs.

I get myself something to eat—a weird meat stew handpie that I heat up on the stove. It doesn't taste right, cold in the middle. I probably should've used the oven. But even in the oven it still would have tasted funny. It's some kind of bologna-type meat, maybe even headcheese, with cabbage and carrots and a dark beef-like gravy. I choke it down anyway.

After several minutes of sitting at the table with nothing to do, the boredom gets to me. I'm not really sure what to do. I pick up my phone and try to go online, but the internet is blocked. I'm not sure how. I can still make calls, though.

I look at Father Adrik's number in my contact list. I wonder if I should call him. I wonder if I should give up on The Trial, give up on Ynaria. She's really a lot different than I thought she would be inside. In fact, she's nothing like I expected, especially after meeting Pavel and Ekaterina. I wonder if she really is the right woman for me. I wonder if humans really are compatible with nesting dolls. I wonder if her father was right. Maybe marrying Ynaria would be a huge mistake.

But I don't call Father Adrik. I'm not ready to give up yet. Instead, I call Mark. Nobody said it was against the rules to call a friend during The Trial. Hopefully, it doesn't disqualify me for cheating.

When Mark picks up, he just says, "Yeah?"

"How's it going, man?" I ask.

"What's up, Ben?" he says. "Haven't heard from you in a few days."

"Yeah, I'm on this trial thing with Ynaria," I say.

"El Douche mentioned something about that," he responds. *El Douche* is what we call our boss at work. "How's it going? Is it knocking some sense into you yet?"

"Well, maybe a little…" I say.

"Really?" A cheerful tone grows in his voice. "So are you going to call the wedding off?"

"No, not yet. But it's pretty rough. Ynaria's inner layers are a *lot* different than I thought they'd be."

"Of course they are. I *told* you."

"No, seriously, you don't understand how different they really are." I look behind me to make sure Ekaterina doesn't hear. I lower my voice. "The one I'm with now is this weird blue squid creature that smells like dead fish. And she's *crazy*. She's the most childish, insecure person I've ever met."

Mark just laughs on the other end.

"It's not funny," I say.

"It's pretty funny," he says.

"I'm trying to hold onto my shit, but it's freaking me the fuck out."

"Look, Ben. Just call it off. You know you don't belong

together. Nesting dolls aren't human. They're unnatural."

"Don't say that," I tell him. "It's offensive."

"But it's true. They were created by alchemists. They are homunculi. There's nothing natural about them."

"Look, I don't care about any of that. I still love Ynaria. I still want to marry her. I just have to get through this trial somehow."

"Do you really want to? Wouldn't you rather spend your life with a normal girl? You know, one that doesn't have monsters living in her?"

"I don't know…" I say.

"Ynaria's the first woman you fell in love with," he says. "It's only natural that you'd *think* she's the perfect girl for you. But are you really in love with her? Can you really love that creature that lives inside of her?"

I don't say anything. I pause, contemplating his words.

He says, "If you hesitate for even a second then you know I'm right."

I shake my head. "I don't know, Mark. I actually really like her second layer. The sex was amazing. It'll be like being married to two super hot women at the same time."

"That's just your dick talking," Mark says.

"I'm just saying it's not all bad. I love her."

"Look, you called me for a reason. You didn't call me to prove to me how much you love Ynaria. You called me because you're having doubts. You called me so that I'd talk you out of it. Tell me I'm wrong."

I think about it for a second. I wonder if he's right.

I thought I was just calling because I was bored, but was I really calling because I don't want to be with Ynaria anymore? Was I calling so that he would tell me it's alright if I gave up on The Trial?

"You're still young," he says. "Way younger than me. If I married the girl I was in love with when I was your age I would've regretted it for the rest of my life. You don't marry that young. It never works out. The vast majority of couples who marry under the age of twenty-five end up getting divorced. Look it up."

I just let out a sigh, not sure what to say.

"Well, I'll think about it," I tell him.

"You better think about it. I'm worried about you."

"Thanks for worrying," I say with absolutely no enthusiasm in my voice.

"I'm going to go grab a beer at the usual place," he says. "If you quit your trial right now you can meet me there. I'll buy."

"I don't know," I tell him. "Don't count on it."

But then I find myself adding, "We'll see."

"Take care, man," Mark says.

"Yeah, take care."

After I get off the phone with Mark, I go back to Father Adrik's phone number and wonder if I really should call him. But something holds me back. No matter what's happened, I still don't want to leave Ynaria. I have no intention of giving her up so easily.

The smell of rotten fish pervades the room and I turn around to see Ekaterina staring at me. Her mouth drops open when she notices the phone in my hand.

"You're calling Father Adrik!" she cries. "I knew it! You're calling off the wedding! You're cancelling The Trial! You hate me!"

I hold up my phone and say, "No, I'm not! I just called Mark."

Tears shower from her eyes. "You called Father Adrik and now you're leaving me!"

"I didn't," I tell her. "Look at my call history."

"But you want to! I know you want to!"

"I don't."

I brave the horrible smell and go toward her, trying to breathe only through my mouth. She slinks down with puppy dog eyes as I approach her. Then I hug her.

"I told your father I'd love all of your layers with all my heart," I tell her. "I meant it when I said that. We will pass The Trial. I won't give up no matter what."

She smiles up at me with wet eyes. "Promise?"

"Yes, I promise."

"Then give me your phone," she says.

I'm not sure why she wants it, but I give her my phone.

She opens up the device and pulls out the SIM card. Then she puts it in her mouth and swallows.

"What the hell did you do that for?" I ask.

The tone of my voice almost makes her cry.

She says, "Now you can't call him until the trial is over."

"But you don't just swallow it. What if that damages your stomach?"

"You'll get it back once you get to my final layer. After The Trial is over."

"That was crazy."

"I'm not crazy…"

I don't know how to respond so I just hug her tightly to my chest, but my squeezes are more out of frustration than love.

Sitting on the couch, I try to comfort Ekaterina as she goes from emotional outburst to emotional outburst.

"So you love me?" Ekaterina asks me. "Even though you think I'm gross?"

"I don't think you're gross."

"But you think I'm too gross to make love to me like you did with my other layers."

"Is sex all that you care about?" I ask. "Every one of you seems to only want to have sex with me. I thought this was about falling in love."

"It is about falling in love," she says. "But sex is important, too. Would you marry someone you've never had sex with?"

"I guess not…"

"You have to fall in love with me both emotionally *and* physically." She's about to cry again. "Otherwise, it doesn't mean anything."

"Well, I didn't fall in love with Pavel physically."

"But you still let him make love to you…"

"Yeah, but I didn't like it. I'd much rather have sex with you than Pavel."

After I say this, I realize I've made a horrible mistake.

"You would?" She smiles up at me with her puppy dog eyes. "So you'll make love to me?"

Before I can say anything, she slithers into my lap, wrapping her tentacles around my waist. With her tentacles spread out, the stench hits me harder than ever. I hold my breath. If I throw up again she'll be so offended that I'll never be able to convince her that I'm not disgusted by her… even though I pretty much am.

Everything inside of me wants to throw her off and run to the bathroom to shower away her stink, but I resist the urge. Instead, I wrap my arms around her and pull her closer. I put my lips on her and kiss her neck.

The taste of her scaly flesh is even worse than the smell. I pull my lips away, spitting out the flavor. Then she puts her mouth onto mine and kisses me. Her tongue oozes into my mouth. But the taste of her saliva is different from the rest of her body. It has a strange oily texture, but it's sweet, like sugar water. It's not at all unpleasant. And her fish-like lips are soft and spongy.

She pulls off my shirt and kisses my chest. Her tentacle hair wiggles in the air like each lock has a mind of its own. It squirms against my body as she licks me.

Her lower tentacles unzip my fly and pull off my pants. They work more efficiently than if she would have done it with her hands. One tentacle curls around my penis and strokes it until it becomes erect, then she pulls me inside her.

She writhes against me, pushing me deep inside. Her voice squeaks and gurgles and moans. She starts crying again, tears flowing down her cheeks and dripping down her chest. But this time the tears aren't because she's upset. She's just overflowing with emotion.

The sensation weakens my sense of smell. I don't feel like I'm going to throw up anymore. She still stinks of dead squid, but it doesn't seem to bother me at this moment.

Ekaterina's breath quickens. She bounces on me faster. Her cries grow louder and higher pitched. The strength of her tentacles gives her better leverage, pushing off the couch and lowering at a speed that a human could never achieve.

Then she cries out, "I'm cumming!"

"Already?" I ask.

Her nipples stretch out of her chest like little fingers. Then they open at the tips like tiny mouths. A thick fluid shoots out of her nipples at me.

"I'm cumming!" she cries again.

The fluid splashes on me, ejaculating out of her nipples in quick bursts.

"What is that stuff?" I cry.

"It's my cum," she says, still writhing against me. "I'm cumming!"

"What?"

As the fluid collects on my chest, it becomes itchy,

then enflamed.

"It burns!" I scream.

I wipe it away, but it only burns me more. Red welts grow on my flesh. The pain overwhelms me and I throw Ekaterina off of me.

"It's like acid!" I cry.

When I look over at Ekaterina, she's frowning, her lips trembling. Then she bursts into tears.

"Waaaa!" she cries. "You don't like my acid cum!"

I reach for a couch cushion and try to wipe it off.

"Why the hell do you have acid cum?" I ask.

She shakes her head, "I don't know! It's just how I cum!"

"It's burning my skin off!"

"Waaaa!" she cries. "My cum burns your skin off! You don't like me!"

"It hurts like hell!" I scream, rubbing melted strips of flesh off onto the pillow cushion.

"You'll never like me!" Ekaterina screams.

Then she slither-runs upstairs and locks herself in the bathroom again.

I rush to the kitchen sink and splash water against my skin, rubbing the burning fluid off of my body.

"Jesus fuck…" I say.

The stuff has burned so deep that it's likely to leave scars on me for the rest of my life.

For days, Ekaterina won't leave the bathroom or talk to me at all. I make her meals and leave them outside her door, but she won't take them unless I'm asleep. I spend most of my time downstairs, sitting on the couch, wondering what I've gotten myself into. The burns on my chest have swelled into puffy strips and I think they're getting infected. They itch constantly. Who knows what kind of weird alien bacteria was in that stuff? I'll probably have to go to the hospital when this is all over. I probably would already be there if I was still able to use my phone.

There's only one bathroom and Ekaterina won't let me in. I haven't showered in days. I have been urinating in the sink and shitting in garbage bags in the basement. It's very unpleasant. I've tried asking Ekaterina to let me use the bathroom, but she won't let me in.

I feel trapped. I wonder if Father Adrik will eventually come and let us out if we stay this way for long enough. I can't call him without the SIM card in my phone. I can't get the front door open. I don't know what to do.

When I sleep, I hear her sobbing and slapping her tentacles against the door. I'm not able to fall unconscious for very long before the sounds wake me up. It's almost like she doesn't want me to sleep. But I don't know what to say. Whenever I try to speak through the door, she just cries out loud, drowning out my words.

I don't understand it. She burned *me*. She scarred *me*. Why is she the one who's so upset? I didn't do anything to her. I've done everything I could to make her happy.

If she doesn't come out soon I think I'm going to go crazy.

Not knowing what else to do, I decide to write messages to Ekaterina and slide them underneath the bathroom door. I write her love poetry. I write messages about what she means to me. I describe how much I liked kissing her, but don't mention that it is the only good thing about making love to her. She still doesn't come out. She reads everything I give her. I can feel her grabbing at the messages when I slip them under the door. She cries less and less every day. But nothing I say is good enough to get her to talk to me face to face.

I stand in front of the door. I can't take it anymore. My patience has completely worn down. This is my last attempt.

I say, "Okay, Ekaterina. Come out now or I have no choice but to call it all off. It's been days. I'm not going to wait any longer."

There's no response from within. Her sobs go to silence, but she doesn't answer.

"I'm serious," I tell her. "I want to marry you, but you won't even talk to me. We're never going to pass The

Trial if you just shut me out. I love you… or at least I *want* to love you, if you'd let me try."

I wait for a response. It's just quiet for several minutes. I almost walk away but then there's a rustling sound. The doorknob unlocks. Then Ekaterina peeks her head out at me. The fishy smell seeps out, more pungent than ever, causing my eyes to water. But I don't back away. I don't even hold my breath.

"You don't hate me?" she asks.

I tell her, "No, but I hate the way you always think I hate you."

The firm tone of my voice doesn't upset her for some reason. It was the first time I was honest with her that didn't make her cry.

"So you're not mad I burned you?" she asks.

"Hell yeah I'm mad about that," I say. "You should have told me you ejaculate acid from your body. I could have worn something to protect my skin. We can't have a real relationship if we don't communicate this kind of information."

She lowers her eyes. "I'm sorry…"

I nod. "It's okay. I forgive you. Now come out of there."

I hold out my hand and pull her upright until she's standing up on her lower tentacles. I take her out of the bathroom and lead her into the room, then sit her down on the bed next to me.

"Look…" I tell her, staring firmly into her black pool eyes that swell with every word I say. "I *do* think you smell bad sometimes. I *do* think you look weird. I *do* think you're kind of gross."

As I say this, her mouth widens. Her eyes tear up so much that they are about to flood her entire face. Before she bursts into a wailing cry, I hold my finger up to her lips and beg her to hear me out.

I say, "But none of that matters. I don't care about any of it. I don't have to like every single thing about you. That's what real love is. You accept each other's flaws. It's okay if sometimes we're grossed out by each other. You said you hate the smell of my farts. You probably think I smell in other ways as well. But you look past that because it's not important. I'm not perfect. I don't have to think you're perfect, either. If our relationship is going to work, we have to make it work. It's not going to be easy. Maybe I'll get burned sometimes." I reach up to my chest and touch the welts beneath my shirt. "Maybe you'll get upset with me. But I'm not going to stop loving you over little things like that. You mean too much to me."

Ekaterina hiccups. Tears fall down her face. But she holds herself back from letting out the biggest cry of her life.

"But…" she says. "But—"

Before she can say anything, I pull her to me and kiss her. We make love again, but this time she lies on her back so that her acid doesn't fall onto me. Her smell is stronger than ever, but for some reason it doesn't repulse me anymore. It smells less like dead squid and more like roasted eel, which I actually think is a kind of delicious flavor if I'm in the right mood for it.

That's what I think about Ekaterina. She's not my favorite layer of Ynaria, but she's kind of the most adorable if I'm in the right mood for her. She's definitely one that I'll never forget.

"Okay, I'm ready to reveal my next layer," she says with a big smile on her face.

I nod in agreement. She's spent enough time as Ekaterina. It's time to continue The Trial. My boss is going to be pissed that I'm taking this much time off of work. Ekaterina was only the halfway point. There's still three to go.

"Are you ready?" she says.

"Yes, I can't wait," I say.

She rubs the crease in her abdomen and begins to separate herself. Inside, I see black reptilian skin. Then two claws with razor-sharp nails slide out and grip the edges of her stomach. It rips itself out of her. Ekaterina's empty husk flies into the air. When it hits the ground, I'm staring at a slimy black creature with glowing red eyes.

I only see it for a second. It opens its mouth with metal pointed teeth and hisses at me. Then it flies out of the room, knocking me backward onto my ass. I hear it screeching and hissing down the hallway.

Then it is gone.

CHAPTER FIVE

???

"What the fuck was that?" I scream at Ekaterina's empty husk, as the black creature disappears somewhere in the house.

I slam the bedroom door and turn the lock, then hold all of my weight against it. That thing wasn't a layer of Ynaria. It couldn't be. That thing was some kind of feral demon.

But the more I think about it, the more I realize that I have to accept the truth. That thing is really an inner layer of Ynaria. She really has a horrifying demonic creature living inside of her.

"Fuck this…" I say, shaking my head.

I'm sorry, Ynaria, but this has gone too far. I can't take it anymore. Pavel and Ekaterina were bad enough. But this thing? There's no way I can marry a woman with this thing living in her. What the hell is it, anyway? It's like something out of my worst nightmares. Mark and Rick were right. Nesting dolls are way too fucked up. I don't know what I was thinking when I fell in love with Ynaria. She isn't natural.

The wedding is over. This trial is off. It's not about

whether I can pass the test anymore. It's about whether I can survive it.

The lights flicker and then go out. I'm left in total darkness. Without any windows, no amount of light can get inside. I'm completely blind. The power must have gone out. And the only way to turn it back on is if I go into the basement.

"The dark's fine," I say. "I'll just stay in the dark."

But the screeching and hissing noises echoing through the house below me tell me that there's no way I want to stay in the dark with that thing all night long.

I don't have the guts to go down into the basement, so I just lie in bed and try to sleep. But there's no way sleep is happening. I can't get the thought of that creature out of my head, the way its glowing red eyes glared at me.

What was Ynaria thinking when she agreed to do The Trial with me? She had to know one of her layers was this creature. She had to know how dangerous it would be for me. Her father had to have known. The priest had to have known—that's why he had me sign the waiver. They knew that I might not make it out of this alive.

Several hours pass. The thing hasn't tried to get in. I wonder if I could just stay here until Father Adrik comes to get me out. He'll find me huddled in a corner in the dark, shaking my ass off. It's better than feeling my way through the dark and into the basement to get the lights back on. It's better than facing the horrific creature downstairs and trying to convince it that I'm in love with it. Does that thing even understand English? Could I even communicate with it if I tried?

No, there's no hope. I'm fucked. I should just accept that. There's no way this is going to work out for me. I never should have gone on The Trial. I never should have thought Ynaria and I were right for each other.

Staying in the bedroom wouldn't be so bad if the lights were on. There's no food up here, but at least there's a bathroom. There's water. I could hold out here for a long time. Maybe Ekaterina even left behind some of the food that I made for her.

"Wait a minute," I say to no one in particular. "I might have a light."

I feel around my nightstand, trying to find my cell phone. I'm not able to call anyone on it—which *really* would be useful right about now—but it's got a flashlight that still might work.

When I find my phone, I turn it on. There's not much battery power. Only a third of the way full. But I've got light. I turn on the flashlight and the room brightens.

"Okay, that's better," I say.

But the light isn't going to last long. I'm not sure what I should do with it. I can have light in here for an hour or so, or I can use the flashlight to go down into the basement and turn the electricity back on.

"No fucking way am I doing that," I tell myself.

But if I'm going to leave the room without someone coming to save me, this is my only chance. Now is the only time.

I unlock the door and step into the hallway. The building is quiet. There's no sign of the black creature. I don't hear the hissing and shrieking noises that filled the place earlier.

"Please don't hurt me," I plead to the hallway, hoping that it will reach whatever part of Ynaria belongs to the beast.

Shining my light down the hallway, I notice massive claw marks on the walls. There's also a black oily fluid smeared across the tile floor and ceiling. How the hell did it get on the ceiling?

I take careful steps down the hallway, shining my light in every corner. When I get to the top of the stairs, I hear shuffling noises down in the living room, like something large is scurrying across the floor.

"I love you," I tell the darkness. "You can change now."

But I know that's not going to do anything.

I shine the light down the stairs, but I see nothing except black oily footprints. I take a step down. Then I pause, listening for the creature. It's silent. I take another step.

"Please let me pass," I say. "I just want to turn the

lights on. Don't you want the lights on?"

My voice echoes. It's like I'm speaking to an empty room.

At the bottom of the stairs, I shine my light in every direction, but the room is empty. I go into the kitchen. The refrigerator door is open. Food is thrown across the tile floor. The thing must have been hungry. Packages of meat have been torn open and dumped all over the floor. I tiptoe to the refrigerator and close the door. Then I grab a butcher knife from a drawer. I don't think the knife will have any effect on the thing, but I feel safer with it in my hand. It's better than being unarmed.

I go to the front door. If I could just get out that would be the best solution. I don't want to go in the basement. I can't wait for Father Adrik to let me out. If I could just get this door open I'd be able to get away.

I slam my weight into the door, but it won't budge. The thing is sealed tight. I jab the knife into the crack and try to pry it open. It doesn't help. I'm not getting out. If there was a sledgehammer I'd just smash my way through a wall, but the closest thing to a sledgehammer I have access to is a wooden meat tenderizer. I won't get far with just a meat tenderizer.

"Okay…" I say, turning around and leaning my back against the front door.

I have no choice but to go down into the basement

and turn the power back on. With any luck, I won't run into the thing.

But as I walk through the living room, shining my flashlight everywhere I look, I realize that there are only two places the creature might be lurking. It's either in the morgue-like room with Ynaria's husk, or it's down in the basement where I need to go. The doors to both places are slightly ajar. There's a good chance it went into either one of them.

I decide to take the chance and go right for the basement. It's likely not the smartest decision I've made in my life, but I guess I've been full of bad decisions as of late. I might as well keep with the trend.

Opening the basement door wider, I shine my flashlight down the steps. I don't see anything but the concrete floor.

"I'm coming down," I say. "Let me pass, please."

I realize that I keep talking to the thing as if it has some kind of intelligence. I guess I'm hoping that it still is like Ynaria in some way. Not because I still think there's a hope of us being together, but because I probably won't be killed if there's a part of her in there.

Pointing the butcher knife forward, I take two steps down into the basement. It's completely silent. No sign of the thing anywhere. Perhaps I got lucky. Perhaps it isn't hiding in the basement after all.

But just as I think this, black fluid drips down onto my neck and arms. I look up. The creature is hanging from the ceiling, looking down at me with its red glowing eyes.

I scream as the thing claws at me. It cuts through my arm, spraying blood onto the wall. I drop the butcher knife,and it falls through the steps. The creature hisses into my face and jumps over the railing, disappearing deeper into the basement.

Gripping my arm, trying to hold in the geyser of blood, I run back upstairs. Fuck the lights. I need to get out of here.

I run upstairs, back into the bedroom, and shut the door.

There's no way I'm going back downstairs no matter what happens.

A few more days pass. I clean my wound and stitch it up with a sewing kit Ynaria brought with her. I keep my phone off as much as possible to save battery power. There's no sign of Father Adrik. I wonder how long he'll wait before coming to get us. I wonder what Mark is thinking, or Ynaria's parents, or even El Douche. They probably know The Trial is going on far longer than it should. I wonder if they'll think about calling the police.

I've gone way too long without food. I have to eat. I feel like I'm going to die unless I have something soon. I tried eating some of the old food Ekaterina left in the bathroom, but it made me sick. I threw up for a full day. Now I'm weaker than ever.

There's no other choice. I have to go back downstairs. I have to get something to eat or else I'll probably starve to death. The last time I was down there, I was able to get to the refrigerator without incident. Maybe I can go down there and gather up enough food to last me for a whole week. That is, if it hasn't rotted from the lack of power.

I use the last of my phone battery to shine the light downstairs. The battery light is blinking. I only have minutes, so I don't waste a second. I rush down the steps, slipping in a puddle of black ink at the bottom of the stairs. Then I go for the kitchen.

There's no sign of the creature, not a single sound coming from the living room as I tear open the cabinet and grab a box of crackers. I didn't realize how hungry I really was. I don't even wait until I get back upstairs before I rip it open and shove a handful of saltines into my mouth. It dries out my saliva and I'm barely able to chew it properly, but I eventually gulp it all down. Then I gather all the food I can into my arms, including a can opener for eating cold stews and soups. I use my teeth to hold my cell phone to brighten the way.

When I leave the kitchen, the light shines into the living room and I see the creature on the floor. I step slowly toward the staircase, wondering if it is getting ready to attack me. But it doesn't move. There's no red light glowing from its eyes.

I wonder if it is asleep or even dead. The thought of it dying sends a panic through my mind. What if it hurt itself? What if it starved to death? If it died then that means that Ynaria will die, too. She can't survive without all seven of her layers.

As I shine the light on the black figure, I realize that it's not dead or sleeping. It's hollow. It's just a husk. The thing must have opened up and released the next layer.

But why did it open? I'm supposed to fall in love with every layer before it will open to the next, but I obviously didn't fall in love with that thing. Why did it change? And where is the next layer?

I put down my stack of food on the dining table, feeling slightly safer with the creature no longer lurking in the shadows. Then I shine my flashlight into the living room, looking for what Ynaria has become.

At first, there's nothing I can find that could possibly be the next layer. The room is empty. There's no sign that anything has been in here for days. But then I see something out of the corner of my eyes. I shine the flashlight onto the wall, high on the ceiling.

There's a large black bug up there, clinging to the white surface, its antennae wiggling in the air. It's bigger than a golden retriever and looks like some kind of cross between a cockroach and an Asian stink beetle.

"You've got to be shitting me…" I say when I see the bug.

Ynaria isn't just a horrific demonic creature. She has also been a giant bug this whole time. What the fuck is wrong with Matryoshkans? How can they have such disgusting things inside of them?

It's a good thing I did go on The Trial. If I married Ynaria without knowing what was inside her I would have regretted it for the rest of my life.

Since the bug doesn't seem to move from the wall, or do anything whatsoever, I decide it's safe enough to go down into the basement and get the power back on before my phone's battery goes dead.

The power box is all scratched up when I get to it. The creature must have done this on purpose, trying to turn the power off. Perhaps it was sensitive to the light. I hit the switch and the lights come on. I guess it wasn't completely damaged from the creature's attack.

When I get upstairs, I eat everything I can that doesn't need cooking—crackers, raw noodles, pickles, apple sauce, I even open up a can of mutton stew and chug it down like a blue raspberry slurpee.

Having not eaten in days, the food is a shock to my body. I get dizzy. I sit down on the couch and take deep breaths, falling in and out of consciousness. When I look up at the giant bug on the wall, it just twitches its antennae at me. It hasn't moved an inch since I've come downstairs. It seems fine. It won't bother me. I just need to get some sleep. I haven't been able to sleep in days. The stress has finally caught up to me.

My eyes roll open as I feel the insect's antennae wiggling against the back of my neck. I'm too weak to move. I let it be. My eyes roll shut.

When I regain consciousness again, I don't know if it's been minutes or hours. The insect is crawling into my lap like a dog. It curls up around me. I want to push it off. I want to get up and go upstairs. But I'm too tired.

The thing purrs against me like a giant disgusting cat. I feel it vibrating through my skin. Without thinking, I put my hand on its back and pet it. The thing is fuzzy. It feels like velvet. When I stroke its back, it purrs louder. The vibration is relaxing. It makes me even sleepier. I close my eyes and go back to sleep.

As I rest, I dream of wonderful things. I dream of living with Ynaria and getting a house together. I dream of holding her in our own bed, feeling her heart beat against my chest. I dream of spending the rest of my life with her.

I pet the humming bug in my lap as I go in and out of consciousness. It's strangely comforting. The thing is so disgusting, so hideous, but it's also warm and soft. I could sleep with it in my arms for days.

I wake to the giant insect cracking open. It separates in my arms. The top half of it rolls off of my lap onto the floor. The lower half slides off onto the middle couch cushion.

A small girl is now in my arms, curled up in a fetal position. She's no larger than a two-year-old, with bright red skin, a bald head, and a plump belly. She doesn't move, resting in my lap. Her warm touch is comforting, even more comforting than the bug's.

The feeling of having her in my arms puts a smile on my face. I don't know why. It's like she radiates a pleasant, euphoric feeling. Then I realize this is the last one, the final layer. This is Ynaria's core. I've made it. After this, The Trial will finally be over.

The girl blinks open her eyes and looks up at me. Her eyes are golden yellow. They shine up at me so brightly that I have to squint.

Without moving her mouth, she says, "Hello, Benjamin."

It's like she's speaking with me telepathically. I can hear her in my mind. It's a gentle, comforting voice.

She says, "I am Dominika and I've been waiting a very long time to meet you."

Then she smiles at me. But she doesn't use her lips to smile. It's like her entire body radiates a smile at me and it's so bright that I can feel it glowing through every inch of my being.

CHAPTER SIX
DOMINIKA

The small glowing woman unfolds in my lap and sits down next to me. She's so light that it feels like she floats on the air as she switches positions. I don't feel like she's even real. I wonder if I'm still dreaming.

"You're not dreaming," she tells me with her mind.

She pulls my phone's SIM card from her mouth and places it on the table.

"How can I hear you?" I ask her. "Are you telepathic? I didn't know Matryoshkans were telepathic."

She continues speaking without moving her lips. "I'm not telepathic. I'm only able to speak to you this way because our souls are connected. My soul is speaking straight into yours."

"I don't understand."

I feel her hug me. A warmth spreads through my entire body. But she doesn't move an inch. It's like she can embrace me on the inside.

"We're soul mates, Benjamin," she says. "We belong together. If we weren't then I wouldn't be able to speak to you like this. I wouldn't be able to touch you with my soul."

I shake my head. "That's impossible. We're not soul mates. I don't believe there's such a thing as soul mates. I failed The Trial. If the door wasn't boarded up I would have left."

She embraces me again with her warmth. Then she says, "You wouldn't have left. You would have changed your mind and come back. Maybe you convinced yourself that you wanted to abandon your path, but deep down it was not what you truly wanted. I can see into your soul and know you were determined to pass The Trial no matter what it took."

I say, "But what was that creature you became? Or that insect? I was scared to death."

With one look, Dominika burrows deep into my eyes. She says, "That was Oksana and Sveta. When I'm Oksana, I just like to be left alone. You don't have to do anything for me then. To prove your love for me, you just had to let me be. I'm sorry I hurt you in the basement, but you were holding a knife. I just acted in self-defense."

I feel warmth cover my wounds, soothing them. They don't heal or anything. It's not like Dominika is actually magical. But her touch makes me feel better. She makes the pain go away. Love can make any pain go away.

Dominika continues, "When I'm Sveta, I don't want to talk or even think. All I want to do is snuggle. Through all these days of The Trial, snuggling you as Sveta was probably the most satisfying. Maybe you slept through most of it, but it made me very happy."

I nod at her. The bug was disgusting and weird, but

it was relaxing and pleasant. If I slept with Sveta in my arms every night I don't think I'd ever have another bad night's sleep for my entire life.

"So, you see," Dominika says, "you passed every test. You proved your love to every layer of me."

"But what about you?" I ask her. "Don't I have to prove my love for you as well?"

I feel her smile radiate through me.

"You don't have to prove anything to me," she says. "The entire Trial was all about getting to me, to my core. If you got to me and we did not have the connection that we do now, then you would have failed. No matter how much my other layers liked you, you still would have failed. But our connection was powerful and instantaneous. There's nothing that can stop us from being together now. Not my parents, not your friends, not anyone in the world. Even *we* couldn't prevent it if we tried. We are helplessly, hopelessly destined for each other."

I nod. Then a smile spreads across my face. I can't believe it worked. I can't believe it's over. We actually passed The Trial. We can actually get married.

"But it's not over yet," she tells me.

I look at her with a questioning face.

She explains, "There's still one more layer beneath me. It's a layer that only I know about. Ynaria doesn't know about it. Vera doesn't know about it. Only I do."

"How is that possible?" I ask.

"Because it's new. It wasn't inside of me a year ago. It's my new core, the new heart of my soul. And I want you to be the first person to see it."

I look into her glowing eyes and nod my head.

"Are you ready?" she asks me.

When I tell her I am, she wraps me up in the biggest glowing hug I've ever felt in my life. Then she begins to separate.

"Do you need help?" I ask her, as she struggles to open herself. Being the innermost layer, she's obviously never been opened before. I can feel the agony spread through her whole being as she tears herself in half.

When it's over, Dominika's halves fall gently against the cushions. And lying in her place, there is a small pink ball coated in milky fluid. Its limbs unravel and I realize what it is. The final layer isn't what I expected. It's not a layer of Ynaria at all. It's a baby. *Our* baby.

I had no idea Ynaria had been pregnant all this time. I knew Matryoshkans gave birth differently than human girls. I knew they didn't show the same signs of pregnancy. There's no swelling or noticeable hormonal changes. And I knew that nesting doll birth control wasn't as effective with human mates as it was with Matryoshkan partners. I knew that we ran a high risk of this happening, but we were in such love with each other that we threw caution to the wind. Still, I never thought we would have a family so soon.

I pick the infant up into my arms and look down into its deep purple eyes as they blink open for the first time. It curls its fingers around my thumb and widens its mouth, staring up at me like I'm the biggest, most majestic and important being that's ever existed.

Then it lets out a cry so loud that it swallows all other sound in the room.

I put Ynaria back together one layer at a time, even Oksana—who slides gently back into Ekaterina without ripping my throat out, despite the look in her eyes. Every layer weeps at the sight of our baby girl in my arms. Every one of them kisses me with happiness, excited for our future. Even Pavel can't believe that he's actually a mother now.

When she's back to her full self again, Ynaria takes our baby in her arms and cradles it to her chest. She can't stop smiling at me. She's just as shocked as I am.

"What should we call her?" I ask.

Ynaria looks into the baby's eyes. Then she says to me, "It's customary to name your first child after the person who brought you together as a couple. So we should name her after your friend, Mark."

The idea sends a cringe down my spine.

I shake my head. "No way. Not Mark. He would *hate* that. Besides, Mark is a boy's name."

Ynaria smiles and looks down at the child. "We'll call her Markie. I think it's cute. Don't you think it's cute?"

When I look down at the little girl with big purple eyes shining up at me, I can't help but agree. "Yeah, it's kind of cute. Markie it is."

Ynaria rests her head on my shoulder, staring down at our child. She can't take her eyes off of it. Neither can I.

I don't think we ever will.

When Father Adrik comes to let us out of the sanctuary, he nearly falls over in shock at the sight of our baby.

"Where the heck did that come from?" he asks, smiling. "You weren't in there *that* long, were you?"

Ynaria nods with a smile on her face. "It was a surprise for both of us."

"Sounds like The Trial was a monumental success," he says. "Everyone at the church will be overjoyed. We'll be talking about this for decades."

But not everyone is as happy as the priest when they find out the results of our trial. Ynaria's father is pissed. He looks like he wants to pound me to death with his giant round body the second I see him. Her mother is ecstatic to meet her new granddaughter, but ignores me completely, pretending that I had nothing to do with it. And my friends are the least happy of them all. They apologize to me when they learn that I have a new child. They react like I've told them I have terminal cancer or something.

The wedding is as big and long and expensive as Ynaria wanted it to be. I have no idea how we're going to pay it all off, but there's no way I would ever want to give her anything less than exactly what she dreamed of. My parents attend, bringing along their young boyfriend that I really didn't like having to sit next to at our rehearsal dinner. They are as annoying and self-absorbed as ever. They take lots of pictures of themselves with their granddaughter so they can put them on their Instagram account. They talk about maybe moving back to The States, but I really hope they don't.

Rick and Mark come as my groomsmen and make fun of me relentlessly for wearing my stupid Matryoshkan clothes that Ynaria forced me to wear. They have no idea what strings I had to pull so that they didn't have to wear outfits just as ridiculous as mine. Both of them have a good time, though. They drink more than anyone else at every wedding event throughout the week. They dance with every Matryoshkan girl they meet, but don't dare sleep with any of them even when they seem interested. After how easily Ynaria became impregnated, they have yet another reason to be frightened of nesting dolls.

After the honeymoon ball, Ynaria and I go on a long trip to the Bahamas, leaving little Markie with her grandparents. Thankfully, Matryoshkan honeymoons are even longer than their weddings. We're able to spend several weeks on vacation and let the rest of the world melt away. For days, I go on romantic dates with Ynaria, have crazy sex with Vera, play late night poker with Pavel, soak in the hot tub with Ekaterina, snuggle with Sveta and bask in the glow of Dominika. The only layer I don't see at all is Oksana, but our honeymoon is all about spending time with each other and Oksana has no interest in spending time with anyone.

I could have given up on Ynaria during our time in The Trial. I could have left her at the first sign of unpleasantness, the first sign of disgust or horror. But that's no way to love someone. Love is just as ugly and annoying and scary and disgusting as it is beautiful and sexual and comforting and fulfilling. Part of me wishes I was Matryoshkan so that Ynaria could've gotten to know me as intimately as I got to know her during our trial. But another part of me knows that it doesn't matter. I don't have to be a nesting doll for that. She'll peel all of my layers off soon enough.

BONUS SECTION

This is the part of the book where we would have published an afterword by the author but he insisted on drawing a comic strip instead for reasons we don't quite understand.

I somehow managed to succeed at turning writing into a career, but soon after going full-time I learned that there are many other small problems about being a writer that I wasn't quite prepared for.

The first time it happened, I was more than ecstatic.
You wrote my favorite book!
You're my best friend forever!
You can have all your groceries for free!

But after about the thirteenth time, it starts to become more awkward than exciting.
You wrote my favorite book!
unshaven
slobby clothes
Umm... Thanks...
Do you know where the toilet paper aisle is?
mustard stain

And sometimes it can even be downright embarrassing.
Hey, *Haunted Vagina* guy! You should write a book called *Haunted Penis* next! Write about penises goddamnit!
Pretending not to notice
Sauce all over face

I totally appreciate all the people who read my books, but I tend to be a pretty introverted person who's not used to being "on" every time I leave the house.

Another thing I wasn't prepared for is how difficult it is to come up with clever personal messages whenever I'm asked to sign a book. Author friends of mine like Jeremy Robert Johnson, John Skipp, and Brian Keene always seem to be able to write messages that are witty and insightful at the drop of a hat. But I never know what to say.
BIG MEAT

Whenever I sign a book for a reader, I usually write messages like:
Hey,
how's it going?
Did you see the new
Punisher series on
Netflix?
I thought it
was pretty good.
– Carlton
Mellick III
STACKING
DOLL
Carlton Mellick III

Or something like:
I haven't eaten at Taco Bell in a
long time. I know the food is
terrible, but every once in a while
I can really go for a meximelt or
one of those fucked up Mexican
pizza things. And what the hell
ever happened to the chilito?
That was the best thing they had.
They should really bring it back.
– Carlton
Mellick III
STACKING
DOLL
Carlton Mellick III

My fingers are made of candy corn! The cast of Star Trek: The Next Generation should have their faces on money instead of any of those asshole presidents! To this day, I still scream in terror whenever I see the sun-baby from Teletubbies!

– Carlton Mellick III

There's also nothing more embarrassing than having someone read your lame message you wrote for them while standing right in front of you.

I also find it difficult when I'm asked to speak on panels at writing conventions. I'm not someone who can talk at length on any given subject.
So what do you do to get yourself inspired to write, Carlton?
First, I write down all the ideas I have in my head and organize them in multiple lists from most marketable to most stimulating to most likely to be multi-layered works of art. Then I read every book I can find on the subject. I interview several people that I envision to be the perfect characters for my book and follow them around for weeks until I get down all the intricacies of their complex personalities. When I'm ready to write, I boil up a pot of imported chamomile tea and sit in front of the fireplace just soaking in the atmosphere, building up all of the creative energy inside of me before I write even a single word.
I just play with GI Joe action figures until I come up with an idea and then I write it.
HIP NEW AUTHOR
FAMOUS AUTHOR
MODERATOR
CM3

So, yeah. Being a writer is way harder than I ever thought it would be, for reasons I didn't even imagine before I started.
Stacking Doll
What the fuck is your problem!
Stacking Doll

You're complaining about how hard it is to sign books and deal with fans who praise you in public.
Oh, boo hoo! Your life is soooo hard!

You wouldn't understand. My life is super complicated.

You're just humble-bragging, aren't you?
Also, it takes like two whole hours to drive to the beach house where I write all my books.
Somebody should kill you.

And I have no room left in my Lake Oswego townhouse to put all this free stuff my fans keep sending me.

Seriously, you deserve to die.

THE END

ABOUT THE AUTHOR

Carlton Mellick III is one of the leading authors of the bizarro fiction subgenre. Since 2001, his books have drawn an international cult following, despite the fact that they have been shunned by most libraries and chain bookstores.

He won the Wonderland Book Award for his novel, *Warrior Wolf Women of the Wasteland*, in 2009. His short fiction has appeared in *Vice Magazine, The Year's Best Fantasy and Horror #16, The Magazine of Bizarro Fiction,* and *Zombies: Encounters with the Hungry Dead*, among others. He is also a graduate of Clarion West, where he studied under the likes of Chuck Palahniuk, Connie Willis, and Cory Doctorow.

He lives in Portland, OR, the bizarro fiction mecca.

Visit him online at **www.carltonmellick.com**

ALSO FROM CARLTON MELLICK III AND ERASERHEAD PRESS

www.eraserheadpress.com

QUICKSAND HOUSE

Tick and Polly have never met their parents before. They live in the same house with them, they dream about them every night, they share the same flesh and blood, yet for some reason their parents have never found the time to visit them even once since they were born. Living in a dark corner of their parents' vast crumbling mansion, the children long for the day when they will finally be held in their mother's loving arms for the first time... But that day seems to never come. They worry their parents have long since forgotten about them.

When the machines that provide them with food and water stop functioning, the children are forced to venture out of the nursery to find their parents on their own. But the rest of the house is much larger and stranger than they ever could have imagined. The maze-like hallways are dark and seem to go on forever, deranged creatures lurk in every shadow, and the bodies of long-dead children litter the abandoned storerooms. Every minute out of the nursery is a constant battle for survival. And the deeper into the house they go, the more they must unravel the mysteries surrounding their past and the world they've grown up in, if they ever hope to meet the parents they've always longed to see.

Like a survival horror rendition of *Flowers in the Attic*, Carlton Mellick III's *Quicksand House* is his most gripping and sincere work to date.

HUNGRY BUG

In a world where magic exists, spell-casting has become a serious addiction. It ruins lives, tears families apart, and eats away at the fabric of society. Those who cast too much are taken from our world, never to be heard from again. They are sent to a realm known as Hell's Bottom—a sorcerer ghetto where everyday life is a harsh struggle for survival. Porcelain dolls crawl through the alleys like rats, arcane scientists abduct people from the streets to use in their ungodly experiments, and everyone lives in fear of the aristocratic race of spider people who prey on citizens like vampires.

Told in a series of interconnected stories reminiscent of Frank Miller's *Sin City* and David Lapham's *Stray Bullets*, Carlton Mellick III's *Hungry Bug* is an urban fairy tale that focuses on the real life problems that arise within a fantastic world of magic.

THE BIG MEAT

In the center of the city once known as Portland, Oregon, there lies a mountain of flesh. Hundreds of thousands of tons of rotting flesh. It has filled the city with disease and dead-lizard stench, contaminated the water supply with its greasy putrid fluids, clogged the air with toxic gasses so thick that you can't leave your house without the aid of a gas mask. And no one really knows quite what to do about it. A thousand-man demolition crew has been trying to clear it out one piece at a time, but after three months of work they've barely made a dent. And then there's the junkies who have started burrowing into the monster's guts, searching for a drug produced by its fire glands, setting back the excavation even longer.

It seems like the corpse will never go away. And with the quarantine still in place, we're not even allowed to leave. We're stuck in this disgusting rotten hell forever.

THE TERRIBLE THING THAT HAPPENS

There is a grocery store. The last grocery store in the world. It stands alone in the middle of a vast wasteland that was once our world. The open sign is still illuminated, brightening the black landscape. It can be seen from miles away, even through the poisonous red ash. Every night at the exact same time, the store comes alive. It becomes exactly as it was before the world ended. Its shelves are replenished with fresh food and water. Ghostly shoppers walk the aisles. The scent of freshly baked breads can be smelled from the rust-caked parking lot. For generations, a small community of survivors, hideously mutated from the toxic atmosphere, have survived by collecting goods from the store. But it is not an easy task. Decades ago, before the world was destroyed, there was a terrible thing that happened in this place. A group of armed men in brown paper masks descended on the shopping center, massacring everyone in sight. This horrible event reoccurs every night, in the exact same manner. And the only way the wastelanders can gather enough food for their survival is to traverse the killing spree, memorize the patterns, and pray they can escape the bloodbath in tact.

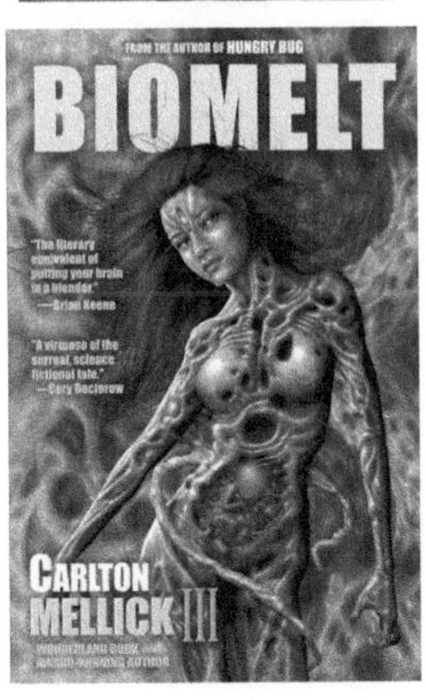

BIO MELT

Nobody goes into the Wire District anymore. The place is an industrial wasteland of poisonous gas clouds and lakes of toxic sludge. The machines are still running, the drone-operated factories are still spewing biochemical fumes over the city, but the place has lain abandoned for decades.

When the area becomes flooded by a mysterious black ooze, six strangers find themselves trapped in the Wire District with no chance of escape or rescue.

EVER TIME WE MEET AT THE DAIRY QUEEN, YOUR WHOLE FUCKING FACE EXPLODES

Ethan is in love with the weird girl in school. The one with the twitchy eyes and spiders in her hair. The one who can't sit still for even a minute and speaks in an odd squeaky voice. The one they call Spiderweb.

Although she scares all the other kids in school, Ethan thinks Spiderweb is the cutest, sweetest, most perfect girl in the world. But there's a problem. Whenever they go on a date at the Dairy Queen, her whole fucking face explodes.

EXERCISE BIKE

There is something wrong with Tori Manetti's new exercise bike. It is made from flesh and bone. It eats and breathes and poops. It was once a billionaire named Darren Oscarson who underwent years of cosmetic surgery to be transformed into a human exercise bike so that he could live out his deepest sexual fantasy. Now Tori is forced to ride him, use him as a normal piece of exercise equipment, no matter how grotesque his appearance.

SPIDER BUNNY

Only Petey remembers the Fruit Fun cereal commercials of the 1980s. He remembers how warped and disturbing they were. He remembers the lumpy-shaped cartoon children sitting around a breakfast table, eating puffy pink cereal brought to them by the distortedly animated mascot, Berry Bunny. The characters were creepier than the Sesame Street Humpty Dumpty, freakier than Mr. Noseybonk from the old BBC show Jigsaw. They used to give him nightmares as a child. Nightmares where Berry Bunny would reach out of the television and grab him, pulling him into her cereal bowl to be eaten by the demented cartoon children.

When Petey brings up Fruit Fun to his friends, none of them have any idea what he's talking about. They've never heard of the cereal or seen the commercials before. And they're not the only ones. Nobody has ever heard of it. There's not even any information about Fruit Fun on google or wikipedia. At first, Petey thinks he's going crazy. He wonders if all of those commercials were real or just false memories. But then he starts seeing them again. Berry Bunny appears on his television, promoting Fruit Fun cereal in her squeaky unsettling voice. And the next thing Petey knows, he and his friends are sucked into the cereal commercial and forced to survive in a surreal world populated by cartoon characters made flesh.

SWEET STORY

Sally is an odd little girl. It's not because she dresses as if she's from the Edwardian era or spends most of her time playing with creepy talking dolls. It's because she chases rainbows as if they were butterflies. She believes that if she finds the end of the rainbow then magical things will happen to her--leprechauns will shower her with gold and fairies will grant her every wish. But when she actually does find the end of a rainbow one day, and is given the opportunity to wish for whatever she wants, Sally asks for something that she believes will bring joy to children all over the world. She wishes that it would rain candy forever. She had no idea that her innocent wish would lead to the extinction of all life on earth.

TUMOR FRUIT

Eight desperate castaways find themselves stranded on a mysterious deserted island. They are surrounded by poisonous blue plants and an ocean made of acid. Ravenous creatures lurk in the toxic jungle. The ghostly sound of crying babies can be heard on the wind.

Once they realize the rescue ships aren't coming, the eight castaways must band together in order to survive in this inhospitable environment. But survival might not be possible. The air they breathe is lethal, there is no shelter from the elements, and the only food they have to consume is the colorful squid-shaped tumors that grow from a mentally disturbed woman's body.

AS SHE STABBED ME GENTLY IN THE FACE

Oksana Maslovskiy is an award-winning artist, an internationally adored fashion model, and one of the most infamous serial killers this country has ever known. She enjoys murdering pretty young men with a nine-inch blade, cutting them open and admiring their delicate insides. It's the only way she knows how to be intimate with another human being. But one day she meets a victim who cannot be killed. His name is Gabriel—a mysterious immortal being with a deep desire to save Oksana's soul. He makes her a deal: if she promises to never kill another person again, he'll become her eternal murder victim.

What at first seems like the perfect relationship for Oksana quickly devolves into a living nightmare when she discovers that Gabriel enjoys being killed by her just a little too much. He turns out to be obsessive, possessive, and paranoid that she might be murdering other men behind his back. And because he is unkillable, it's not going to be easy for Oksana to get rid of him.

CUDDLY HOLOCAUST

Teddy bears, dollies, and little green soldiers—they've all had enough of you. They're sick of being treated like playthings for spoiled little brats. They have no rights, no property, no hope for a future of any kind. You've left them with no other option-in order to be free, they must exterminate the human race.

Julie is a human girl undergoing reconstructive surgery in order to become a stuffed animal. Her plan: to infiltrate enemy lines in order to save her family from the toy death camps. But when an army of plushy soldiers invade the underground bunker where she has taken refuge, Julie will be forced to move forward with her plan despite her transformation being not entirely complete.

ARMADILLO FISTS

A weird-as-hell gangster story set in a world where people drive giant mechanical dinosaurs instead of cars.

Her name is Psycho June Howard, aka Armadillo Fists, a woman who replaced both of her hands with living armadillos. She was once the most bloodthirsty fighter in the world of illegal underground boxing. But now she is on the run from a group of psychotic gangsters who believe she's responsible for the death of their boss. With the help of a stegosaurus driver named Mr. Fast Awesome—who thinks he is God's gift to women even though he doesn't have any arms or legs--June must do whatever it takes to escape her pursuers, even if she has to kill each and every one of them in the process.

VILLAGE OF THE MERMAIDS

Mermaids are protected by the government under the Endangered Species Act, which means you aren't able to kill them even in self-defense. This is especially problematic if you happen to live in the isolated fishing village of Siren Cove, where there exists a healthy population of mermaids in the surrounding waters that view you as the main source of protein in their diet.

The only thing keeping these ravenous sea women at bay is the equally-dangerous supply of human livestock known as Food People. Normally, these "feeder humans" are enough to keep the mermaid population happy and well-fed. But in Siren Cove, the mermaids are avoiding the human livestock and have returned to hunting the frightened local fishermen. It is up to Doctor Black, an eccentric representative of the Food People Corporation, to investigate the matter and hopefully find a way to correct the mermaids' new eating patterns before the remaining villagers end up as fish food. But the more he digs, the more he discovers there are far stranger and more dangerous things than mermaids hidden in this ancient village by the sea.

I KNOCKED UP SATAN'S DAUGHTER

Jonathan Vandervoo lives a carefree life in a house made of legos, spending his days building lego sculptures and his nights getting drunk with his only friend—an alcoholic sumo wrestler named Shoji. It's a pleasant life with no responsibility, until the day he meets Lici. She's a soul-sucking demon from hell with red skin, glowing eyes, a forked tongue, and pointy red devil horns... and she claims to be nine months pregnant with Jonathan's baby.

Now Jonathan must do the right thing and marry the succubus or else her demonic family is going to rip his heart out through his ribcage and force him to endure the worst torture hell has to offer for the rest of eternity. But can Jonathan really love a fire-breathing, frog-eating, cold-blooded demoness? Or would eternal damnation be preferable? Either way, the big day is approaching. And once Jonathan's conservative Christian family learns their son is about to marry a spawn of Satan, it's going to be all-out war between demons and humans, with Jonathan and his hell-born bride caught in the middle.

KILL BALL

In a city where everyone lives inside of plastic bubbles, there is no such thing as intimacy. A husband can no longer kiss his wife. A mother can no longer hug her children. To do this would mean instant death. Ever since the disease swept across the globe, we have become isolated within our own personal plastic prison cells, rolling aimlessly through rubber streets in what are essentially man-sized hamster balls.

Colin Hinchcliff longs for the touch of another human being. He can't handle the loneliness, the confinement, and he's horribly claustrophobic. The only thing keeping him going is his unrequited love for an exotic dancer named Siren, a woman who has never seen his face, doesn't even know his name. But when The Kill Ball, a serial slasher in a black leather sphere, begins targeting women at Siren's club, Colin decides he has to do whatever it takes in order to protect her... even if he has to break out of his bubble and risk everything to do it.

THE TICK PEOPLE

They call it Gloom Town, but that isn't its real name. It is a sad city, the saddest of cities, a place so utterly depressing that even their ales are brewed with the most sorrow-filled tears. They built it on the back of a colossal mountain-sized animal, where its woeful citizens live like human fleas within the hairy, pulsing landscape. And those tasked with keeping the city in a state of constant melancholy are the Stressmen-a team of professional sadness-makers who are perpetually striving to invent new ways of causing absolute misery.

But for the Stressman known as Fernando Mendez, creating grief hasn't been so easy as of late. His ideas aren't effective anymore. His treatments are more likely to induce happiness than sadness. And if he wants to get back in the game, he's going to have to relearn the true meaning of despair.

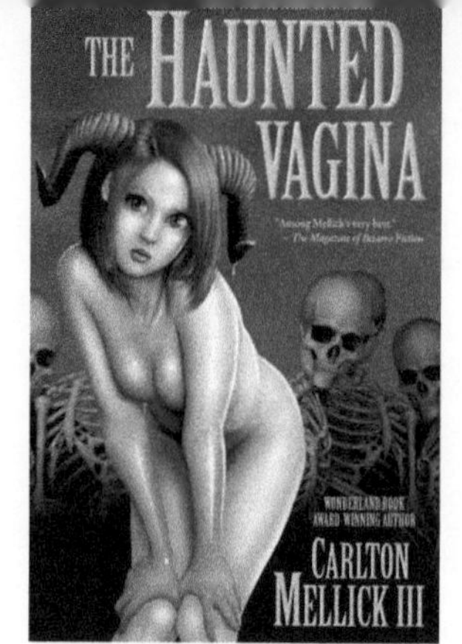

THE HAUNTED VAGINA

It's difficult to love a woman whose vagina is a gateway to the world of the dead...

Steve is madly in love with his eccentric girlfriend, Stacy. Unfortunately, their sex life has been suffering as of late, because Steve is worried about the odd noises that have been coming from Stacy's pubic region. She says that her vagina is haunted. She doesn't think it's that big of a deal. Steve, on the other hand, completely disagrees.

When a living corpse climbs out of her during an awkward night of sex, Stacy learns that her vagina is actually a doorway to another world. She persuades Steve to climb inside of her to explore this strange new place. But once inside, Steve finds it difficult to return... especially once he meets an oddly attractive woman named Fig, who lives within the lonely haunted world between Stacy's legs.

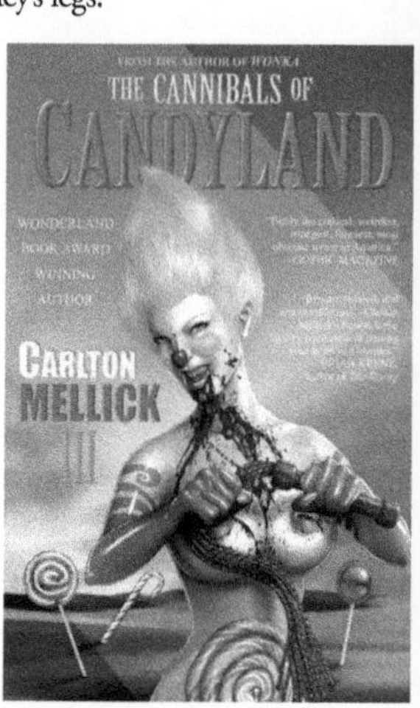

THE CANNIBALS OF CANDYLAND

There exists a race of cannibals who are made out of candy. They live in an underground world filled with lollipop forests and gumdrop goblins. During the day, while you are away at work, they come above ground and prowl our streets for food. Their prey: your children. They lure young boys and girls to them with their sweet scent and bright colorful candy coating, then rip them apart with razor sharp teeth and claws.

When he was a child, Franklin Pierce witnessed the death of his siblings at the hands of a candy woman with pink cotton candy hair. Since that day, the candy people have become his obsession. He has spent his entire life trying to prove that they exist. And after discovering the entrance to the underground world of the candy people, Franklin finds himself venturing into their sugary domain. His mission: capture one of them and bring it back, dead or alive.

THE EGG MAN

It is a survival of the fittest world where humans reproduce like insects, children are the property of corporations, and having a ten-foot tall brain is a grotesque sexual fetish.

Lincoln has just been released into the world by the Georges Organization, a corporation that raises creative types. A Smell, he has little prospect of succeeding as a visual artist. But after he moves into the Henry Building, he meets Luci, the weird and grimy girl who lives across the hall. She is a Sight. She is also the most disgusting woman Lincoln has ever met. Little does he know, she will soon become his muse.

Now Luci's boyfriend is threatening to kill Lincoln, two rival corporations are preparing for war, and Luci is dragging him along to discover the truth about the mysterious egg man who lives next door. Only the strongest will survive in this tale of individuality, love, and mutilation.

APESHIT

Apeshit is Mellick's love letter to the great and terrible B-horror movie genre. Six trendy teenagers (three cheerleaders and three football players) go to an isolated cabin in the mountains for a weekend of drinking, partying, and crazy sex, only to find themselves in the middle of a life and death struggle against a horribly mutated psychotic freak that just won't stay dead. Mellick parodies this horror cliché and twists it into something deeper and stranger. It is the literary equivalent of a grindhouse film. It is a splatter punk's wet dream. It is perhaps one of the most fucked up books ever written.

If you are a fan of Takashi Miike, Evil Dead, early Peter Jackson, or Eurotrash horror, then you must read this book.

CLUSTERFUCK

A bunch of douchebag frat boys get trapped in a cave with subterranean cannibal mutants and try to survive not by using their wits but by following the bro code...

From master of bizarro fiction Carlton Mellick III, author of the international cult hits Satan Burger and Adolf in Wonderland, comes a violent and hilarious B movie in book form. Set in the same woods as Mellick's splatterpunk satire Apeshit, Clusterfuck follows Trent Chesterton, alpha bro, who has come up with what he thinks is a flawless plan to get laid. He invites three hot chicks and his three best bros on a weekend of extreme cave diving in a remote area known as Turtle Mountain, hoping to impress the ladies with his expert caving skills.

But things don't quite go as Trent planned. For starters, only one of the three chicks turns out to be remotely hot and she has no interest in him for some inexplicable reason. Then he ends up looking like a total dumbass when everyone learns he's never actually gone caving in his entire life. And to top it all off, he's the one to get blamed once they find themselves lost and trapped deep underground with no way to turn back and no possible chance of rescue. What's a bro to do? Sure he could win some points if he actually tried to save the ladies from the family of unkillable subterranean cannibal mutants hunting them for their flesh, but fuck that. No slam piece is worth that amount of effort. He'd much rather just use them as bait so that he can save himself.

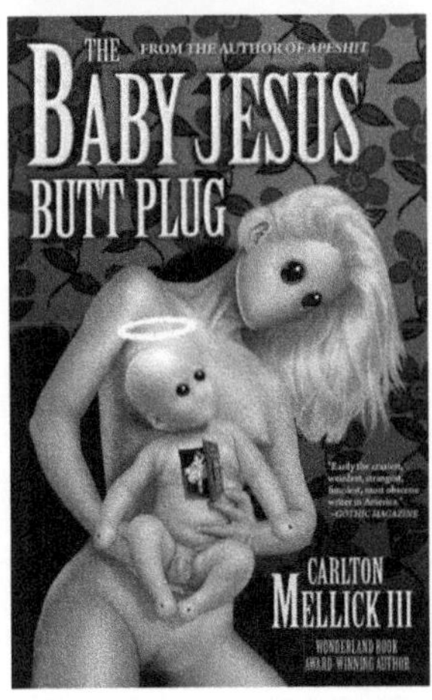

THE BABY JESUS BUTT PLUG

Step into a dark and absurd world where human beings are slaves to corporations, people are photocopied instead of born, and the baby jesus is a very popular anal probe.

Milton Keynes UK
Ingram Content Group UK Ltd.
UKHW042219190924
1731UKWH00001BA/1